He pulled her close and kissed her. Suzanne wanted to struggle against him and resist, but she didn't.

Instead she let herself indulge in the wild, punishing sweetness of his lips, and the hands that pulled her soft curves into his hard form. Rick deepened the kiss and her body felt as if it was on fire. That's when she knew she was in danger, and pulled away.

Suzanne grinned and said in a shaky voice, "I knew you hadn't changed." She tried to make her voice light to lessen the impact of their kiss.

But Rick's smoldering gaze wouldn't let her. "I have changed, Suzanne," he said in a dark voice. "But you're too afraid to believe that."

"Why would I be afraid?"

He took a step toward her.

She held up her hand. "I know you're used to getting what you want, especially from the fairer sex. But let me tell you one thing. All you're getting from me is the house."

"Is that a challenge?"

"It's a warning."

Rick winked. "You should know me better than that. Warnings only make me try harder," he said, then walked down the stairs and left.

Books by Dara Girard

Kimani Romance

Sparks
The Glass Slipper Project
Taming Mariella
Power Play
A Gentleman's Offer
Body Chemistry
Round the Clock
Words of Seduction

DARA GIRARD

fell in love with storytelling at an early age. Her romance writing career happened by chance when she discovered the power of a happy ending. She is an award-winning author whose novels are known for their sense of humor, interesting plot twists and witty dialogue.

When she's not writing she enjoys spring mornings and autumn afternoons, French pastries, dancing to the latest hits, and long drives.

Dara loves to hear from her readers. You can reach her at contactdara@daragirard.com or P.O Box 10345, Silver Spring, MD 20914.

DARA GIRARD

WORDS of Seduction

KIMANI™
ROMANCE

To Shannon and Pamela.
Thanks for everything!

KIMANI PRESS™

ISBN-13: 978-0-373-86155-2

WORDS OF SEDUCTION

Copyright © 2010 by Sade Odubiyi

Recycling programs
for this product may
not exist in your area.

www.kimanipress.com

Printed in U.S.A.

Dear Reader,

Remember *Peyton Place?* With that New England town full of secrets, betrayals and new love? Well, that classic novel became the inspiration for *Words of Seduction.* When I decided to write about a novelist returning to her small town after writing a bestseller, *Peyton Place* became the perfect model to help get my imagination flowing.

So now I'd like to welcome you to Anadale, a sultry Southern town in North Carolina, where a woman who left in disgrace is about to come back and turn the town on its head. She reconnects with a former bad boy, uncovers secrets the town would rather keep hidden and unlocks the truth of her destiny.

This is a story about secrets, seduction and second chances.

So settle back in a comfortable chair and enjoy.

All the best,

Dara Girard

Chapter 1

"Don't be alarmed."

Suzanne Rand spun around with a gasp of surprise. Not because of the words, but because of the voice. *His voice.* She knew it far more intimately than she wanted to. His voice had a deep rumbling tone that made her think of bourbon and jazz and hot summer nights. She stared at the man standing in front of her dressed in worn jeans, a faded shirt and sneakers. In the distance, the sun set, lengthening the shadows of the trees and the large stately white house behind her while the distant cry of a skein of Canada geese flew overhead.

She was all alone with him, one thing she'd never imagined happening again.

"Rick Gordon," she whispered as though if she spoke too loud he'd disappear.

"It's been a long time," he said, his seductive voice washing over her and causing her skin to tingle. Suzanne knew his dark gaze could produce the same effect and much more. She couldn't imagine what he thought of her. She no longer wore her hair in microbraids down her back; instead, her thick black hair was pulled into a French braid. She wore a blue chiffon top, offset with a pair of fitted white linen pants, which showed off her new slimmer figure, and her lips sported bright red lipstick instead of the subdued pink she'd always been known for.

Suzanne folded her arms, suddenly feeling vulnerable under his assessing gaze, wishing for a cool spring breeze or some other reason to go back inside. Yes, it had been a long time, but not long enough and she'd hoped never to see him again. She'd planned to slip in and out of town before having to deal with her past. Stares and whispers had been part of her life when she'd left the small town of Anadale, North Carolina, five years ago. Those stares and whispers had greeted her again, since she'd been forced to return. Meeting Rick Gordon would only make those whispers grow.

"I'm surprised you remember me," he said, his steady gaze piercing into hers.

Suzanne shrugged, trying to appear nonchalant, although inside she was shaking. "You shouldn't be. Everybody remembers you."

A slow grin spread on his face and his eyes brightened with mischief, making his handsome face more appealing. "Especially you?" It was a statement rather than a question, but she refused to respond to it even though he was right.

Rick Gordon was an unforgettable character. She remembered that he was always in trouble or causing trouble for someone else. He was unlike anyone else in town—reckless, rebellious, wild and one of the poorest residents of Anadale. The police knew him, but he never got into serious trouble and had never seen the inside of a courtroom. "He's mine, if he ever comes in front of me," Suzanne's father, Gerald Rand, used to say, keenly aware of his power as a judge. "The courtroom's my kingdom."

That might have been true, but Anadale was Rick's kingdom. He could draw people in with a smile or a look and he had a charisma that was undeniable. Handsome wasn't the first thought that came to mind when one looked at him. Stunning suited him more. From his sharp, confident profile to his magnetic brown eyes. He was coarse, bold and sexy and that hadn't changed. People used to say he could walk into a room and make the temperature rise because he was living with the devil. "You stay away from him," her father had warned. And she had, except for one summer during her senior year. But Suzanne didn't want to remember that now.

There had been so many things she'd wanted to forget about Anadale, but she hadn't forgotten him. Even after he'd left town ten years ago, he'd stayed in her memory. And as his profile grew from trade school dropout to owner of one of the largest energy-saving electronic companies on the east coast, the gossips of Anadale made sure that she remembered him. His success astounded them. No one had expected him to amount to anything. Only a few people knew that as a teenager he created energy-saving devices in his spare time to help heat and light the old dilapidated box house he and his family lived in. Later he developed a business around his creations and continued to use his knowledge to help poor and low-income families use solar and wind energy to save money.

"You look well," he said.

Although his tone was polite, it set Suzanne on edge. What was he doing here? What did he want? "Thank you," she said, using the same formal tone.

He glanced at the camera in her hand. "What are you doing?"

Suzanne blinked at the object in her hand for a moment as though she didn't know how it got there. "Oh, yes." She turned to the house. "I was taking pictures."

"For your scrapbook?"

"No," she said, surprised that he remembered her old hobby. "I don't do that anymore. These are for the new brochure to help sell the house."

"I thought the Realtor was supposed to do that."

"Yes, she did," Suzanne said cautiously. "But we need to create another one."

"Because the first one was crap."

"No," she said, defensive. "that's not it."

Rick pulled out a worn brochure from inside his jacket. "I've got it right here."

"Oh," Suzanne said with a tinge of chagrin. He was right. The brochure was crap. Everything about her return to Anadale seemed to follow suit. Three weeks earlier she'd expected to come back, arrange her father's funeral, settle his affairs then go back to her life. But upon her arrival Suzanne had come to discover that her father had become a stranger. The man who'd once been a prominent judge and upright citizen of the town had turned into a debt ridden, bitter old man who'd lived as a hermit for the past year.

He'd kept this from her. Any time she'd phoned, his voice had sounded upbeat and he told her he was well. Although her mother had died three years ago, Suzanne never worried about her father being lonely. He was a sociable man and always had company. It was only at his funeral that she'd discovered that her father had dismissed his housekeeper and gardener three months before his death without explanation. That he'd stayed holed up in his house for months and hadn't paid his bills and had let all of his investments tank.

Instead of the beautiful home she'd remembered as a child and young woman, she found a dusty tomb that needed to be sold—fast. So she hired Della because she was a Fulford (which meant a lot in Anadale), and came from a proud and established family. Della's mother had been a top-selling Realtor and owned Fulford Realtors, one of, if not the most, successful Realtors in town. So it was inevitable and/or expected that Suzanne would work with them. Unfortunately, Suzanne soon realized that Della had only inherited the "name" but not the skills.

Suzanne soon discovered that Della had created a totally ineffective brochure that was glossy and full of color (and very expensive), but showed *three* images of the living room and only *one* other picture of the backyard. In addition, she hadn't listed the house in the proper venues and had twice missed appointments. However, Suzanne knew she couldn't fire her without the whole town thinking that Suzanne considered herself above them and had become too "New York." So instead she decided to take some new pictures of the house and get them to the printers so that a new brochure could be made and distributed.

"What are you doing with that?" Suzanne asked, looking at the crumbled brochure in his hand.

"I wanted to see what the house looked like," Rick said in a low tone.

She blinked. "Why?"

"The same reason as anyone else."

She furrowed her brow. "I don't understand."

Rick folded his arms with a look of impatience. "Why would someone look at a house?" When she didn't reply he said, "I plan to buy it."

Suzanne schooled her features, determined to hide her surprise and doubt. "Oh. Of course."

The corner of his mouth kicked up in amusement. "You don't believe me?"

"No, it's not that," she said quickly. "I'm sorry, Della, I mean Ms. Fulford, didn't tell me she had someone coming by."

He shrugged, unconcerned, a casual gesture that made it clear that the problem wasn't his. "She told me to come by."

"Right." Suzanne fumbled for her cell phone, desperate to have a reason not to look at him. Did he mean it? He wanted to buy her house? Why? What was he up to? It was at moments like these that she wished she still had Neena the housekeeper. Neena would always help her deal with situations she didn't want to. She dialed Della's number. After four rings Della picked up and

Suzanne heard noise in the background—like that of a blow-dryer. "Della, did you forget that you had an appointment today?"

"What?" Della shouted into the phone.

Suzanne glanced up at the sky for patience. "Did you have an appointment today?"

"I don't think so."

"A Mr. Rick Gordon?"

"Rick!" Della squeaked. "I forgot about him. I'm so sorry. I scheduled my hair appointment late and I needed to get my roots done. You must think I'm a dingbat to forget such a delicious specimen of a man. I know he's a Gordon and totally off-limits to women like us, but he's still a danger to any woman who wants to keep her reputation clean, if you know what I mean. Have you seen him lately?"

Suzanne sent Rick a quick glance hoping he couldn't hear what Della was saying over the phone, but from the look he sent her she knew he'd heard every word. She lowered her voice. "I'm looking at him right now."

"What?"

Suzanne reluctantly raised her tone. "I said I'm seeing him right now."

"You mean he's there?"

"Yes."

"Alone with you?"

"Yes."

"You lucky—"

"Della!"

"I'm almost done. I'll be right over. Say in fifteen minutes. Can he wait?"

Suzanne gripped the phone. Wait? Della wanted him

to wait? What was she supposed to do with him? She turned to him and lifted an eyebrow in question. "Do you mind waiting?"

He shook his head.

"I'm not sure how long she'll be," Suzanne lied, hoping to discourage him.

"That's fine."

She silently groaned then returned to Della. "Yes, he'll wait."

"Great. I'll be right over. Don't let him get away. Toodles."

Suzanne closed the phone, determined not to repeat Della's signature sign-off. "Let's wait inside," she said, then headed for the house before he could disagree.

He didn't move. "Not that way."

She turned to him, surprised. "What way?"

He glanced at the side door. "Don't you think I deserve front door treatment? Or am I not good enough yet?"

"I always go through the side door."

"But you don't take guests that way."

Suzanne gritted her teeth at his smug tone and implication that she was being a snob. Unfortunately, he was right. She never took guests through the side entrance.

She took a deep calming breath then changed her direction and went around to the front, where the house sported a grand entrance with four large pillars and a solid oak door with stained glass. She opened the door then made an exaggerated display of welcoming him inside.

Rick ignored her mockery and stepped into the large foyer. He slowly turned in a circle as he looked around.

As he studied the interior of the house, Suzanne studied him. She couldn't help herself. He was a man who commanded attention without effort. His large, solid form had not been diminished by the years, but enhanced. His massive shoulders stretched the fabric of his shirt and his muscular legs could put tree trunks to shame. That coarse air about him had been slightly tamed, however, because although his clothes looked worn, she could detect that they were of a fine quality.

"Wow, never imagined it would look like this," Rick said in awe. Without invitation, or wiping his shoes on the welcome rug, he walked directly into the living room and sat down on a large green sofa. One thing was clear—Rick was here to stay.

Chapter 2

Suzanne stood in the hallway wishing Della would come soon. She resisted the urge to look at her watch because she knew that would only make her more anxious. What was she supposed to say? Do? Was he really interested in the house? Why? He didn't seem the type to want to settle down. What did he really want? She watched him sitting on the couch looking the complete opposite of the moneyed businessmen who'd visited before.

He looked like a handyman who'd lost his way and didn't care. She noticed something glitter on his wrist and saw his watch. It wasn't a gold plated imitation, but the genuine thing. At that moment, Suzanne decided to hone in her thoughts. She had to remember that what he looked like didn't matter. He had money and right now money was what she needed. "Would you like something to drink?"

He rested his arm along the back of the couch. "No."

"Something to eat?"

"I'm fine."

She sighed then sat on the off-white love seat in front of him. She could use a drink, but she wouldn't show weakness if he didn't. She'd match his nonchalant arrogance. Unfortunately, she didn't know where to look. He was like an elephant in a closet—hard to miss—and her gaze kept returning to him. Finally, her glance fell on the book resting on the side table near him. *Beneath the Ashes* by Suzanne Rand. She quickly looked away hoping he wouldn't notice it there. He did. At first he merely glanced at it, then picked it up. "Ah, your book," he said as though he'd made an amazing discovery.

She shifted awkwardly in her seat. "Yes."

"Made you rich I hear." He flipped the book over.

Suzanne had been taught that it was vulgar to talk about money so she made a noncommittal sound.

He took it as an agreement. "And happy."

She cleared her throat, but it remained dry. "I was pleased to have accomplished something."

"Hmm. Others weren't so amused by your accomplishment."

Suzanne sat back determined not to be offended. "Did you read it?"

Rick raised his brows, impressed. "That's an interesting question."

"Why?"

"I'm surprised you think I can read."

"Yes," she replied in a dry tone. "I expected you'd learned how to read, but I'm sure your father didn't teach you." Suzanne regretted the words the moment they left her. She knew how much he hated his father.

A dark look passed over his face, but quickly disappeared. When he didn't speak, Suzanne crossed her legs and swung her foot, desperate to break the silence. "So, have you read it?"

"No, I haven't."

She felt herself relax. "Good."

He sent her a piercing look that raised the hairs on the back of her neck. "Is there a reason I shouldn't?" He flipped through the pages, but not in a quick careless motion. He was slow and deliberate, forcing her to look at his hands. She didn't want to, but couldn't help herself. She remembered his hands the most. They were callused and large yet tender when they touched her. And at one point in her life she'd let him touch her everywhere. "Anything about me in here?"

The sound of his voice startled her out of her dangerous thoughts. She swallowed and said with a bit more force than she'd planned, "It's a story. Fiction. Nothing more."

"That doesn't answer my question."

"I don't plan to answer your question."

"Why?" he challenged.

"Because I made the story up."

"Not all of it."

"Most of it."

He shot her a glance. "A clever excuse to air our town's dirty laundry."

"I don't deny that I based some of the events listed

in the book on things that have happened here, but Anadale's laundry is no dirtier than any other town's."

"So you say," he drawled, "and I know better than to argue with a judge's daughter so I'm not going to disagree with you."

"Although you want to?"

"I want to do a lot of things," he said in a silken tone, "but that doesn't mean I'll follow through."

Suzanne brushed imaginary fuzz from her trousers to keep her trembling fingers occupied.

Rick opened the book again and looked at the professional photograph on the inside jacket flap then glanced up at her. "You look better in real life."

"Thank you," Suzanne said, not caring if his statement was an insult or a compliment.

He snapped the book closed then set it down. "You're a little skinny, though. Don't you like the food up North?"

"I like to stay toned."

He nodded but looked unconvinced.

Suzanne glanced around the room, a room whose every crevice she knew by heart, uncrossed her legs and crossed them again, wishing she could think of something else to say. Finally she decided to be blunt. "So why are you really back in town? Are you here to make some husband or boyfriend nervous?"

Rick tilted his head to the side, his clever eyes making it clear that he knew her attempts to provoke him wouldn't work. He flashed a wicked grin. "I could say the same about you and the wives."

She stiffened. "What do you mean?"

"Some wives and girlfriends aren't too happy with your return."

"But I don't have your reputation."

"You may not have left with much of a reputation, but you've certainly come back with one."

"I'm surprised anyone noticed."

His smile grew and she felt her face grow warm as he continued. "You expected them to and you succeeded in getting their attention with your flashy sports car and stylish clothes." His gaze swept her body with admiration. "Congratulations."

Suzanne hated how close to the truth he was. She had come back wanting to show the town that she was no longer the pathetic housewife she'd been five years ago. She should have been used to their whispers and stares, but they still bothered her. As a young girl they whispered about her because she was the judge's perfect daughter, years later they whispered about her because she was attorney Wallace Lyon's perfect wife. Then the whispers turned to pity when it became clear that Wallace preferred the attention of other women besides his wife. Then came the divorce. She had left town in shambles, but now she was back.

"My days of making trouble are over," Rick said with a sincerity that surprised her.

"You're ready to settle down," she said, unconvinced.

"Something like that. Have you seen Lyon?"

She scowled at the sound of her ex-husband's name. "Yes, at the funeral."

He nodded. "Sorry to hear about your loss."

"About as sorry as a fish forced to live on dry land," she sniffed. It was no secret how Gerald Rand and Rick Gordon felt about each other.

He shrugged. "I'm not saying I'm sorry he's dead. I'm

saying I'm sorry for your loss. In that I'm being genuine."

"How's your mother?" Suzanne asked. She didn't care, but she knew it was polite to ask.

Rick raised an eyebrow, amused by her feigned interest. "She's fine." He glanced around the room, drumming his fingers on the couch.

Suzanne glanced at her watch. *Where was Della?* It felt like hours had passed, although in reality it had only been ten minutes since she had spoken to her.

Rick noticed the motion. "Do I make you nervous?"

"No, I just hate to see you waiting."

"I bet you hate seeing me at all."

Suzanne narrowed her eyes, but didn't respond.

Rick leaned forward, resting his arms on his knees. "I know you're too polite to admit it, but I know it galls you, doesn't it? You can't stand the thought of trash like me going through your fine house."

"Stop it," she said in a tight voice.

"I'm polluting your fine walls."

Suzanne jumped to her feet. "I said stop it. Or you can leave right now."

He stood in front of her. "I'm not going anywhere."

"Then I will."

He seized her wrist, his dark eyes boring into hers with a ruthless sheen. "It doesn't matter what you think of me because money changes everything. It evens the score."

"Only on the lowest level," she shot back. "Because there are levels you'll never reach."

"One day that pedestal you're sitting on is going to fall, Suzanne, and you'll have no one else to look down on."

She narrowed her gaze. "And if you think money and class is the same thing, you're going to learn a hard lesson." At that moment, they were standing so close to each other, Suzanne could feel his breath on her skin, and could see the artery in his neck pulse.

"You pretend to have a lot to say. So how come you haven't written a second novel?" he asked, his dark eyes probing deeper into her soul.

The sound of screeching tires stopped Suzanne's reply and Rick released his hold. They heard a door slam then Della raced into the house. Her years of salon care were clearly evident. Della's black hair had been expertly curled and styled, her nails were finely manicured and her face glowed with moisturizer and expertly done makeup. "Sorry, I'm late. Are you ready to have a look around?" While Della could not be called beautiful, she was a very striking woman, who knew exactly what colors to wear to accentuate her honey baked skin, and what fashions suited her ample frame.

Rick turned to her. "Yes."

"Suzanne, don't you want to come with us?" Della said when Suzanne returned to her seat. She turned to Rick. "She knows so much about the house."

Rick looped his thumbs in the belt hole of his jeans. "I guess she has more important things to do than try to convince someone to buy her house," he said sarcastically.

Suzanne met his look. "If someone needs to be convinced, perhaps they shouldn't look."

"No harm in looking."

"Yes, that's right," she said with a brittle smile. "It's free."

Rick's jaw tightened and for a moment Suzanne wondered if she'd pushed him too far.

"But the house isn't," Della said, oblivious to the tension between them. She walked up to Suzanne and whispered, "Please help me with this one. You know I wouldn't ask if I didn't mean it." Her voice went lower still. "But this man makes me weak in the knees."

Suzanne wanted Della to earn her commission, but knew that wasn't going to happen. "All right."

Della smiled in relief. She turned to Rick. "She's so good at telling stories."

Rick kept his gaze on Suzanne. "So I've heard."

Della clapped her hands together, pleased. "Come on. This will be fun." She walked past him and headed down the hall.

Rick remained in the doorway and motioned Suzanne past him. "After you," he said with the same mocking gesture she'd used earlier to usher him inside the house.

Suzanne bit the inside of her mouth then turned sideways and began to squeeze past him.

Rick noticed the attempt and smiled. "I remember a time when you didn't mind touching me."

Suzanne halted and looked up. She shouldn't have; his penetrating gaze impaled her and she smelled the faint intoxicating scent of his cologne. She steeled herself against it. "That time has passed."

"Really?" he said in a low voice. "Do you have many lovers up North?"

"That's none of your business."

"Doesn't stop me from asking."

She turned away. "Let me show you the kitchen," she said, then walked toward it.

"Can it take a lot of heat?" Rick asked.

Suzanne sent him a look over her shoulder. "Even the devil would find comfort."

"That sounds good to me."

Suzanne gave them the obligatory tour, which was made difficult by Della's trivial comments.

"Oh, Suzanne, don't forget to point out the hand-stenciled tile in the kitchen," Della piped in as though it was of utmost importance. "And don't forget to tell Mr. Gordon about all of the recent updates, like the sanding of all the wood floors, and replacement of the broken guest room window."

Suzanne cringed. Those upgrades hadn't been done in years. When she was showing Rick the main bathroom on the second floor, Della pointed out that the toilet might be "too low to the ground" for a tall man, such as himself, and that he may want to put in a higher one. "We all spend so much time in this little room," Della said with a bright grin. "We need to make sure it's comfortable."

Suzanne stifled a groan.

Della noticed Suzanne's pained expression and tried to make the room sound more pleasant. "But I'm sure it's easier for men, you just aim and—"

Suzanne yanked her out of the room before she could finish. "Let's go to another section of the house," she said, then showed them the all-purpose room where she and her mother did crafts. She'd been forced to learn to do needlepoint. "A lady is of no use if she can't crochet or needlepoint," her mother liked to remind her. She showed them the five bedrooms, leaving her bedroom for last. She quickly tidied up. "I didn't expect company," she said, pulling up the sheets of her unmade bed.

"I'd always wondered what this room would be like," Rick said lifting a bra from off the back of her chair.

Suzanne snatched it from him. "As you can see there's plenty of space." But somehow he made the room feel small, and the bed, the most prominent object in the room. She shoved her bra in a drawer. "Let's go."

Next she showed them her father's study and the family room. Throughout the tour Rick remained attentive. At times, a little too much so. Suzanne wasn't sure if it was real or fake, but she didn't care. She wanted it to end. Finally, after approximately forty minutes, Suzanne flopped into a white wicker couch on the wrap-around porch outside and watched, with relief, as Rick and Della left. Although she desperately wanted the house to sell, Suzanne secretly hoped Rick was leaving for good. That this was the last time she would see him, and that the invisible thread that somehow bound them together would be broken for good.

Chapter 3

"So what did you think of the house?" Frieda Gordon asked her son the moment he entered the house. She tapped the ashes of her cigarette into a nearby tray and set her shrewd gaze on him.

Rick sat on the plastic-covered leather sofa in his mother's living room and smiled, satisfied. "It's perfect."

"And Suzanne? You must have had an opinion of her."

Yes, he certainly had an opinion. Several in fact and they all bothered him. Suzanne Rand, the judge's daughter, the attorney's wife, and now the successful novelist. But all those labels didn't seem to suit her. There was something different about the woman he'd just met. There was a steel edge to that Southern polish she'd perfected. A hardness he wanted to break. He knew a side to her that no one else had seen and she could pretend what had happened that summer had just been a fling, but he was going to remind her that it was something more. That *he* was something more. Something more than just the poor kid she'd decided to toy with for a couple of months out of boredom and then discard.

The boy she never once invited inside her house, or introduced to her friends or parents. He was her delicious secret and, for a while, he'd thought it was fine. He didn't mind, he was used to clandestine relationships and had indulged in plenty. By the age of twenty-two he was a pro. He never took girls seriously, but something about Suzanne had been different, and for a moment he thought they had a chance. That what they had was real. But she'd let him know that wasn't true. That he wasn't good enough for her. Now he'd let her know that that had changed.

Frieda dragged on her cigarette and narrowed her gaze. "Be careful there," she said, as though she'd read his thoughts.

Rick rested his arm on the length of the couch and dared her to challenge him. Instead his mother reached for her carton of cigarettes and held them out to him as a peace offering. "Wanna smoke?"

"I quit, remember?"

"When?"

He sighed, annoyed. "Five years ago."

"Oh, yeah." She puffed on the cigarette, taking the smoke into her mouth and then exhaling. "Now I remember. I didn't realize it'd been that long."

Rick stared at the smoke as it drifted up to the ceiling. The new house he'd bought her had nine-foot high ceilings, fine wooden floors and the right address. But except for the size, it was still too similar to the cramped house he'd grown up in. Despite the expensive furnishings the place smelled of old cigarettes, stale beer and plastic flowers. It still held too many painful reminders of his past, except for one. He no longer needed to worry about getting his head bashed in by his father.

"Rickie, promise me not to get into any trouble now that you're back here."

He hated when she called him that and she knew it, so he didn't correct her. "Yes, ma'am. I know why I'm here."

"You always had a weakness for women."

"No," he said with a laugh, "they had a weakness for me."

"Is she as pretty as before? Like when she was crowned Miss Anadale?"

"Yes."

"I could have been crowned Miss Anadale once, but her mother beat me out because she was from the right family." Frieda Gordon angrily stubbed out her cigarette. "Even though I was prettier. I was the prettiest girl in town at the time."

Rick knew it was best not to reply. His mother may have been a beauty once, but her hard life, hard drinking and chain-smoking had stripped her of most of her good features. Her once vibrant cocoa skin was now a dull muddy brown, and her notable high cheek bones looked like hollow shells. His mother had long ago resorted to wearing wigs, since her thick black-brown hair, which was her pride and glory, began thinning and falling out. Her hair had been her main source of vanity, and although she was now in her late sixties, she could not let go of her youthful image. As a result she only wore one wig style. Unfortunately for his mother, cascading black, shoulder-length hair was unbecoming and only emphasized how far she was from the beauty she had once been.

"Does Suzanne look the same?"

He tapped a beat on the back of the couch. "She looks like her picture."

"Hmm, so she's skinnier. Not that sad little porky thing she'd become when she married that Lyon boy. Remember when she got married? Oh, wait, you weren't there."

"Yes," Rick said in a distant voice. "I was there." The only reason he'd been at Suzanne's wedding was because he'd been working two jobs that spring and the company he worked for had been hired to set up the equipment for the stage show. A famous singer had been flown in to perform. He remembered the hundreds of guests and Suzanne in a stunning white gown becoming another man's wife.

"Oh, that's right, you left the year after, so you didn't see her change the way I did. Not that I felt sorry for her. She did just like her sort always does—marry for money and prestige, even though everyone knew that boy dropped his pants for anything with breasts and you know what. Did she look happy?"

"Momma," he said with growing impatience. "Her father died only a few weeks ago and she has to sell their house."

A sly grin touched his mother's lips. "And we know why."

Rick rubbed his arm, a feeling of restlessness seizing him. For a moment he wished he were back at 468

Trellis Court surrounded by the fresh smell of flowers, the pristine wood furniture and history. In a way he and Suzanne still lived in different worlds. Although his apartment was nothing like his mother's place, it did not have the casual elegance of 468 Trellis Court.

Frieda waved her cigarette at him. "Don't let her flash and glamour get to you."

Rick glanced at his watch. He tried to make sure that his visits with his mother never lasted more than an hour. "I won't."

"You did once."

"That was a long time ago."

"Yes." She dragged on her cigarette, inhaling until her cheeks looked like they'd stick together. "And you can't trust her. She wrote that filthy book about us. About the whole town. She got rich off of our pain. Keep your distance."

Rick laughed. "Don't try to mother me now. You know I always do what I want to." He stood and went to his mother's bookshelf and took Suzanne's book from it. He looked at the worn spine and battered pages. "I've always wondered why you've read it so many times, if you hate it so much."

"I have my reasons."

He replaced the book. "I'm sure you do. And I have mine so don't worry about me. I'm not interested in her." That was a lie, but he lied well, and his mother sat back and relaxed.

Suzanne stared up at the ceiling of her bedroom, willing herself to sleep. She was still trying to get used to the quiet. She was used to the cacophonous noises of a bustling city and the silence of the town had become foreign to her. But she knew her sleepless night had nothing to do with the sound of crickets. She couldn't sleep because of Rick.

For years she'd tried to convince herself that the time she had spent with him had been a harmless flirtation. A rebellion. That it hadn't meant anything. But now she knew she'd been deceiving herself. No matter how he made her feel, she couldn't succumb again. She knew she had terrible taste in men and her present circumstance proved it. Her father was a bastard leaving her nothing but his debt and memories of his overbearing reputation. Her ex-husband shamed her every day of their marriage by sleeping with any woman who was willing and there were plenty. Then there was John Peckman, her agent. The man she'd at one time thought she was in love with. The man who had helped her get a six-figure contract for her novel and guided her through the shock of sudden fame and fortune. The man who helped her invest in a bad prospect, then developed a drug and gambling habit and ran off with the rest of her money. What a fool she'd been to trust him so completely. She decided she would never trust a man again.

The investigator she had hired couldn't find him and Suzanne soon realized that she was quickly going through the advance for her second novel, and she wasn't close to finishing her next manuscript. Everyone thought she was a rich, successful novelist, but she was nearly broke. She felt like a failure. If she didn't sell the house soon everyone would discover her lie and her shame. She knew she had no other place to go. She'd left her apartment in New York with the rent two months past due.

Had her mother been alive, she wouldn't understand Suzanne's predicament. Leslie Rand believed that a woman should always have a man pay for everything. "Always let a man pay your way," her mother had told her. And she meant in all things from a meal to a mansion. Her mother expected men to take care of women. With a coy smile and a compliment her mother had turned the strongest men into mush. "You use the right words, baby, and any man will be yours," she said.

"The right words?"

"Yes, words of seduction. You seduce them with praise, you feed their ego and let them think your advice comes from their own minds and you'll be indispensable. Your compliments will become like a drug and you'll have them coming back for more. Your power comes down to three things—E.T.W. Eye contact, touch and words. Use those three things in the right manner and no man can resist."

And her mother taught her all that she knew, but she hadn't taught her which men to choose and that men could be betrayers. She preferred to be alone and the only seductive words she used appeared on the page. No man was going to help her out of this situation, but fortunately she had friends and they would come to her aid if she needed them. She knew she'd never be homeless.

One of her best friends, Noreen Webster, had offered her a room in her three-story luxury town house, but Suzanne didn't like that option. Noreen was still reeling from the demise of her marriage and dealing with her unstable sister. Then there was Claudia Madison, her other best friend. Suzanne loved her, but knew she could never live with her. She was too free-spirited for

Suzanne's more conservative ways. No, Suzanne knew she would have to find a way to survive on her own. And there was one thing she knew for sure. She didn't need another man to cause trouble in her life. Once she found a way to get out of this mess she was moving away and starting over.

The next morning Suzanne overslept. She hadn't meant to. She was usually good at keeping to a schedule, but after staying up late last night thinking—or trying not to think—about Rick, the ringing of the alarm clock didn't wake her but the phone did. She pounded the alarm with her fist then grudgingly picked up the receiver.

"Where are you?" an anxious voice said. She recognized the formal Bostonian tone as her friend Noreen's.

She wiped sleep from her eyes. "What?"

"Oh, don't tell me you forgot it."

She sat up alarmed. "Forgot what?"

"The book signing event."

Suzanne jumped up and swore. "That was today?"

"Yes."

Suzanne swore again. The signing was a huge media event with more than twenty authors, including her friends. She glanced at the clock. She had two hours. One hour to get ready and another to get there. She would be cutting it close, but she could make it. "I'll be right there."

"Do you want me to send someone to pick you up?"

"No, I'll be fine. See you soon."

Suzanne quickly changed into a pair of black tailored slacks and a white fitted shirt, then grabbed a bagel with strawberry jam before racing out. But when she took a bite of her bagel some red jam dropped on her top so she had to rush back inside and change into a wrinkled blue blouse she didn't have time to iron. An hour and fifteen minutes later, she raced through the mall, trying to find the author's booth. The event, which was being sponsored by one of the largest book chains in the area and the local writers' association, was an annual event that Suzanne had always attended, since the release of her novel four years earlier.

Right outside the main bookstore, tables and chairs were arranged in a semicircle, sporting larger-than-life silhouette cutouts of fictional characters, several book displays and grinning authors sitting behind tables waiting to sign books. A long line of fans started to form. Book signings were not one of her favorite activities, but Suzanne knew that any amount of publicity would be better than none. She hated the lookie-loos who walked by slowly, just to look at her, and made comments such as:

"She doesn't look very much like her picture."

"I hated her book. I don't know why it sold so well."

And sometimes men would approach with lame lines like "Hello my Nubian princess. I would like to make you my queen" and then slip their phone number to her, expecting her to call.

And, naturally, every author at a book signing expected the following question:

"Do you know where the bathroom is?"

But Suzanne didn't have time to worry about the headaches the day might bring, she needed to find her spot. Fortunately, one of the organizers, a heavyset man named Mr. Whimple who had a thin mustache and a fat bowtie, saw her first and led her to the right place. She sat down at the white covered table where stacks of her books sat off to the side with a supply of pens. She sank into the seat exhausted.

"Are you okay?" Noreen said, coming up to her table with a worried look. Her brown eyes looked large behind her black-framed glasses that matched her equally black suit, which gave her the appearance of an executive. But her unruly curls held back by a patterned cloth headband destroyed that image and made her look like a kid playing dress-up. Her petite size didn't help the matter, but in spite of her youthful appearance Noreen was tough and shrewd and used that shrewd gaze now.

"I'm fine."

"But—"

"You made it!" Another voice interrupted. Suzanne turned and saw her friend Claudia who was dressed in a flowing chiffon dress that draped her willowy frame perfectly. Her black hair fell to her chin and at that moment she could pass for a twenties' flapper. All she needed was a string of long pearls and a thin cigarette. She dashed over and quickly kissed Suzanne on the cheek. "I'm a few tables over, but I had to say hello. You look great."

Noreen frowned. "She looks harried."

Claudia made a face; Noreen ignored her as she studied Suzanne more closely. "It's not like you to miss something this big," she added.

"But I didn't miss it," Suzanne said, wishing Noreen would drop the subject.

Noreen wasn't ready to. "You would have if I hadn't called."

"Yes," Suzanne reluctantly admitted. "I'm glad you did. I had a long night. A lot to think about."

"Like what?"

Suzanne glanced at her watch. "We don't have time to talk about it now."

"Then we'll talk about it later."

Behind her Claudia rolled her eyes. Although Noreen was the youngest amongst them, she deemed herself the leader.

Suzanne forced a smile, she didn't want to talk at all, but she knew Noreen wouldn't let it rest. "Okay."

"Good. And don't even try to sneak away."

"Do you have spies?"

Noreen smoothed out a wrinkle on her sleeve. "I don't think you want to find out," she said, then walked over to her table.

Claudia shook her head. "She's a strange little thing. There's so much I still don't know about her."

"But we love her anyway."

Suddenly, a voice came over the loud speaker. "Authors please get to your tables so we can begin."

"That's my cue," Claudia said. She blew her friend a kiss then left. Suzanne watched her go, again struck by the contrasts of her friends. They were complete opposites in looks and their work. She'd met them four years ago at a national writers' conference in Raleigh. Noreen had relocated to the area because of her husband's job. She was already an established author. Claudia had left her successful psychology practice after her first novel became a bestseller, and was working on her second novel while Suzanne was the un-published newbie.

It was only after she'd checked into the hotel that she'd learned that her assigned roommate wasn't coming and Suzanne couldn't afford the full price of the room. Noreen overheard her talking to the registrar and offered to stay with her even though she lived close by and could have easily gone home. They met Claudia in the hallway as she tried to get into their room with the wrong key. They laughed at the mix-up and had clicked over food and drinks and had been friends ever since.

Noreen was now a top romance novelist whose passionate tales constantly hit the bestseller lists. Claudia's deep family dramas had twice been turned into TV movies and she also used her degree in psychology to pen several bestselling nonfiction relationship books for women. Both women were a lot more prolific than Suzanne, who felt like a one hit wonder in their presence. Her book, *Beneath the Ashes*, had been an un-expected blockbuster and had put her name on the map overnight. But could she write another hit?

Suzanne didn't have much time to wallow in her fears once the signing officially began. For the next two hours she smiled and posed for photos with adoring fans, autographed books and graciously accepted com-pliments. The day would have been perfect if one of her fans hadn't asked the one question she dreaded.

Chapter 4

"When will we see your next book?" the woman asked with an eagerness that was palpable. She blinked as though she were about to cry and trembled with such excitement it seemed possible that the butterfly prints on her shirt were about to fly away.

Suzanne focused her gaze on her inscription. "Soon. Hopefully." She snapped the book closed then handed it back.

The woman leaned closer. "Will it be another book set in Waverly?"

"No. This one will be different."

"How different? I'd love another Waverly story." The five women behind her agreed and then spent the next five minutes telling her about plot points they'd like to see and who should be with whom. "They're all great ideas,"

Suzanne interrupted. "Who knows what the future holds." She continued to smile, wishing them to disappear.

The woman would have continued to press her, but thankfully Mr. Whimple came to her rescue and quickly and effectively shuttled them through the line.

By the second hour everyone's faces became a blur, but Suzanne was careful to make sure that each fan felt as though she thought they were special. And they were, but she felt like a fraud. Her readers thought she was a glamorous rich author. Would they still want her autograph if they knew the truth? That she wrote fiction, lived fiction and had a fictional persona to maintain.

"Hello, Suzanne."

At the sound of her ex-husband's voice, Suzanne nearly snapped her pen in two. She took a deep breath before looking up at him. She wished he'd changed. Gotten fat or thin, or grayed or bald. But he was still tall and good-looking with a smooth charismatic smile that swayed most people into believing he was trustworthy. He was the same handsome bastard she'd divorced five years ago. "Did you get lost?"

"I came to see you. It seemed the only way, since you won't return my calls and pretend not to be home when I stop by."

"You sound paranoid." Suzanne averted her gaze and looked at the anxious ladies standing in line.

"Speaking of paranoid, I haven't seen you in town. Are you hiding?"

"No."

"I know you, honey. You can't lie to me."

"What do you want?" she said through clenched teeth.

"I want to talk to you."

"This is not the place."

"I'm not moving until you promise to see me."

Suzanne snatched the book in his hand and quickly signed it, resisting the urge to write something obscene. She closed the book then held it out to him. "Thank you, sir, now have a nice day."

He shook his head. "I'm not leaving."

Suzanne glanced at the interested faces behind him and groaned. She didn't want to cause a scene. "I saw a diner close by here."

"Nelly's?"

"Yes," she said although she didn't know the name. She'd find it anyway. "I'll meet you there at three."

"Good." He turned to the women behind him. "Sorry for taking up your time, ladies," he said, then walked away, and the women watched him go as though they'd just developed a new crush. Suzanne had to resist snarling.

When the event ended, Claudia raced up to her. "Let's go for drinks."

"I have to see Wallace," Suzanne said, flexing her hand.

"Why?" Noreen asked, joining them.

"I don't know, but I might as well get it over with. We're meeting at Nelly's."

"We've got your back," Claudia said.

Noreen furrowed her brow. "What does that mean?"

"It means that we'll be spying on them from another booth."

"I don't think that's necessary," Noreen said.

Suzanne agreed, but Claudia was already headed in the restaurant's direction. "I want to get good seats," she called back to them.

"I'd better make sure she also gets a good location," Noreen said, then followed her.

Suzanne sighed and walked at a more leisurely pace.

She didn't want to see Wallace again. What did they have to say to each other? She entered the restaurant and saw him flirting with a waitress and groaned. She caught a glimpse of Claudia who was miming a gagging reflex and stifled a grin before heading to Wallace's table. He stood when he saw her.

"Stop being a gentleman," she said, annoyed. "Nobody's watching."

He sat down. "You look good."

"Did you get her number?"

"Who?"

"The waitress."

He frowned, wounded. "I was just being friendly. You're the only one I care about."

Suzanne sat back amazed. Even his lies were the same. "What do you want?"

He sighed. "So much for small talk."

"We're not going to talk at all if you don't get to the point."

"You still hate me," he said with a grin. "That means you care."

Suzanne rested her chin in her hand, bored.

He reached across the table and rested his hand on hers. "Suzanne, it's been so long and—"

She pulled her hand free. "What do you want?"

"How come you haven't remarried?"

"Too busy enjoying those alimony payments."

"I doubt they amount to much compared to what

you're making now. I think there's another reason. You don't want to forget me."

"Wallace," Suzanne said with thinning patience. "What do you want?"

"Besides a second chance?"

She squeezed a slice of lemon into her water. "Yes, besides the impossible."

He rested his forearms on the table and leaned forward. "I've got an idea for a book."

She sipped her drink. "So?"

"I'm willing to give it to you and we could split the proceeds."

"I don't need your idea. Why don't you write it yourself?"

"You know I'm no good with words."

"You're an attorney, you're very good with words."

"I mean putting stories on paper. Don't shoot me down. This could be another bestseller for you. As a lawyer I have seen and heard things that would amaze you."

"Find a ghostwriter. I am not interested in working with you."

"If you're so full of ideas how come you haven't published anything new in years?" he said, his proper Southern drawl taking on a nasty tone.

"Because I've been busy. Not all writers have a book out every year." She scooted to the end of the chair ready to leave. "Is that it? Are we through?"

"I've been thinking about you."

Suzanne shook her head in disgust. "Stop it."

"I'm sorry about your father."

She stood.

He let out a fierce sigh. "Look, I really could use your help."

She sat down intrigued. "Why should I help you?"

"Okay, so I may not have been the best husband, but I did take care of you."

"Your women weren't the only reason I left."

"I know and you wouldn't have been able to write your book without me."

"What?" Suzanne said, shocked.

"I gave you insight that you wouldn't have known otherwise. You're lucky I didn't sue for part of your royalties."

"It's fiction!"

He glanced around nervous. "Keep your voice down."

"You want to sue me?"

"No, honey, but you have to admit that I helped you. There's enough fact in your book to make people nervous."

"I don't know what you're talking about."

"The Lowell case. You based your book on that case, almost every detail was the same except you changed the outcome."

A sense of anxiety gripped her. He was right. She had. *Beneath the Ashes* was a story about how a small, tight-knit community and its key residents dealt with the outcome of a murder trial. She'd had so many mixed emotions about the real murder that had happened in Anadale, but through fiction she'd been able to come up with some answers. She let her anxiety ease. It was still just a story and nothing more. "It's fiction. And that's all."

She stood, but when she moved to leave, Wallace leaped up and grabbed her arm, his hand like a vise. "Don't rush off, Suzanne. I know things that might interest you. If you want more dirt on this town I can give it to you."

"Let go of me."

His grip tightened making her wince. "Not until you agree that you owe me something."

She ignored the pain and glared up at him. "I don't owe you anything."

"Life doesn't work that way. You can't come back into town and think nothing has changed. I heard that Gordon's interested in Trellis Court, but do you know why he's interested?"

"Suzanne, there you are!" Claudia's bright voice broke in. "Come and join us."

Noreen smiled from behind her.

Wallace loosened his grip and Suzanne yanked herself free, rubbing her arm.

Claudia sent him a cool look. "Who is your friend?"

Suzanne made introductions, glad for the reprieve. "Claudia, Noreen, this is Wallace, my ex-husband. Wallace Lyon, better known as 'Who's Wallace lying with now'?"

Wallace's welcoming grin froze on his face.

"Wallace, this is Claudia and Noreen."

Noreen held out her hand. "Better known as her best friends who will hunt you down like a rottweiler if you hurt her."

Wallace shook her hand and put on his Southern charm. "A pleasure, ladies. And you have nothing to worry about. I never hurt the things I treasure."

"For a lawyer you lie very badly."

Claudia shoved Noreen aside. "Ignore her. She's going through a bad divorce." She gently brushed invisible fuzz from his shoulder and Wallace's frozen smile slowly became real. "I can tell you're the type of man women can trust." Before Noreen could protest, Claudia looped her arm through Suzanne's. "But we really have to go and it's been such a long time since we last saw Suzanne so I hope you don't mind if we steal her away?" She didn't wait for a reply. "No, of course you don't. Thank you." She hurried Suzanne over to her table and sat down. "Aren't you glad that we're here?"

"I didn't need rescuing," she lied, with a plastic smile, "but thanks anyway."

"Why did you have to tell him about my divorce?" Noreen said.

"Because you don't insult a man when you want something." She rested her chin in her hand. "Now let's get some food and talk."

Moments later the three women sat with glasses of pink lemonade and an assortment of appetizers. Although Suzanne had found Wallace's request somewhat threatening, she soon dismissed the whole incident from her thoughts.

"So, how are things?" Noreen finally said.

Claudia lifted her drink, a devious smile on her lips. "Better yet, who is *he?*" She looked directly at Suzanne.

Noreen turned to her. "Why do you think it's a man?"

"Only a man would make Suzanne nearly miss a major book signing."

"I'm sure there's another explanation. She's stressed because she has to sell her father's house."

They both turned to Suzanne and waited with expectation.

Suzanne bit her lip, wondering if she should lie, then decided against it. "A man I used to know came by the house yesterday."

"Why?" Noreen asked.

Claudia shook her head as though her friend was crazy. "Because he wanted to see her."

"No," Suzanne said. "He wanted to buy the house." When Claudia looked unconvinced she continued. "You know the guy I told you about? The one I used to know?"

They stared at her blankly.

"My summer incident."

"Rick Gordon?!" the two women said in unison.

"Stay away from him," Noreen said, knowing the reputation Suzanne had shared about him.

"Why?" Claudia countered. "He might be a nice diversion."

Noreen looked at her, appalled. "I can't believe you write books about relationships when you don't know anything."

"I know plenty."

"Which is why you've never married or had a relationship last longer than a year."

"At least I've never been divorced."

"Only because you're too afraid to commit so you choose men who won't commit to you."

Suzanne held up her hands. "Let's not fight about this. Let's just agree that we haven't had the best of success when it comes to men."

"I admit it," Noreen said. "At least I don't advise others about it."

Claudia raised a brow. "You just write love stories you don't believe in."

Suzanne grabbed her handbag. "I don't need this."

"Okay," Noreen said quickly. "We're sorry."

Claudia lowered her voice. "Tell us more about Rick."

Suzanne set her handbag aside. "There's not much to say."

"You had plenty to say when you told us about him last time."

"Only because I was describing the past. It's different now. I know this man and he's not interested in me. He wants property and that's all he came for." *And to let me know that he's still sexy, still dangerous, rich and completely out of reach.* "There's nothing going on. It was just a shock to see him again."

Noreen adjusted her glasses. "A good shock or a bad one?"

"A little of both."

Claudia grinned. "The best kind."

Chapter 5

Suzanne pulled up into her driveway and stared at the lawn in dismay. It needed to be mowed—desperately. Unfortunately, she'd have to do it herself. It didn't matter that she'd never mowed in her life or that grass cuttings made her eyes water. The house was beginning to look like a neglected relic and she knew image was everything. She remembered the days when the gardeners would come once a week to make sure that the bushes were trimmed and the grass was the right height—two inches. Her mother would use a ruler to make sure. Four hundred and sixty-eight Trellis Court always looked perfect and pristine. Not anymore. Dandelions and onion grass sprouted boldly through the soil and the lawn stood at an unruly height of over two inches.

Resigned, Suzanne went to the old shed out back and pulled on a pair of faded overalls over her brightly colored orange tank top and grabbed a disposable paper mask from off the shelf. Initially she tried to work the riding mower, but it wouldn't start so she had to use the gasoline powered one. When she discovered that the mower was empty, Suzanne made a quick trip to the gas station and filled up. It was late afternoon before she got started.

After three attempts to get it started, Suzanne smiled with satisfaction when the mower finally roared to life, and began to cut the grass. She ignored her watering eyes and the fact that her lungs had began to feel tight. All she had to do was the front lawn. She imagined how good it would look when she was done. But after a half hour the mower started to smoke and shake.

"What do you think you're doing?" Rick's angry voice demanded. He pushed her aside and turned the machine off. "Do you know how dangerous that is? This thing is a time bomb."

"Dangerous what is?" Suzanne wheezed, surprised she could still talk.

He stared at her for a moment before suddenly swinging her up in his arms.

She gasped then began to cough. "What are you doing?" she eventually managed to say.

He didn't reply. Instead he took her back inside the house and laid her on the couch. He removed her mask and threw it on the ground. "Why the h—" He took a deep breath before speaking, his tone losing some of its edge. "Why were you mowing the lawn when it's obvious you're allergic to grass cuttings?"

"I—"

He shook his head and swore. "Never mind. Don't talk. I have to take care of you first. Your eyes are swelling shut and your breathing's bad. Let me get you some ice."

Suzanne lay on the couch trying to figure out what was happening. What was he doing there? He remembered that she was always teary-eyed around grass cuttings, but how did he know she was allergic? She had never been diagnosed. Her father had just thought it was her excuse to stay inside and avoid outdoor parties she didn't want to attend. The thought that she was allergic surprised her. But before she could think about it any more Rick returned.

Suzanne felt the shift of the cushions as he sat down. He lifted her head and placed it on his lap. She didn't have the energy to fight him or the comforting feeling that followed his touch. Soon she felt the cool sensation of an ice cube against her lips. "Swallow this to help with the inflammation," he said.

She didn't argue, she was in too much pain and could hardly see him. She didn't want to imagine what she looked like. After a while she didn't care as she felt his large, warm hands on her forehead and another ice cube in her mouth. Soon she let the weight of her exhaustion overcome her and drifted off to sleep.

When she woke up, the room was eerily still. She saw the setting sun cast rays of light through the blinds. She sat up and looked outside and saw Rick's car in the driveway, but she didn't see him. She was about to turn and look for him when she noticed the lawn and her mouth fell open. It was completely mowed. Even the bushes had been trimmed. For an instant she was in the past when Trellis Court was at its full glory. In the background she could hear her mother humming as she arranged a bouquet, and hear her father barking orders over the phone, and smell fresh bread seeping through the kitchen as Neena prepared the evening meal.

"Good, you're up."

Suzanne turned around and saw Rick standing in the doorway wearing only his jeans. His feet and chest were bare as he dried his hair with one of her towels. When she continued to stare at him, he frowned. "Are you upset because I used your shower?"

She pointed out the window. "Did you do that?" she asked, her voice still weak.

He nodded.

"Who did you hire? How much did they cost?"

He looked at her confused. "It was free. I did it myself."

She widened her eyes. "You didn't have to."

"I know."

Suzanne returned her gaze to the window and rested her chin on her hands. She gazed out at the sight, her eyes filling with tears. "That's one of the nicest things anyone has ever done for me."

Rick sat down beside her and smiled in disbelief. "You're being polite." When she wiped a tear away, his smile fell. "You're serious."

"Yes." The men in her life always had others do their work. Not that she minded. That was the way things were done. If you wanted the lawn mowed you hired someone. You always hired someone else to work for you. Even John, her agent, had flowers delivered instead of buying them himself. Rick didn't come from that world. No matter how much money he'd made he'd be blue collar to the core. She thought of the hours it must have taken him and her heart was filled with gratitude. "Thank you."

"It was nothing," he said, a little embarrassed. "I'm glad to see you're looking better."

"I probably look worse than I feel."

His eyes clung to hers and for the first time they weren't glinting with humor or anger or pride, but something tender, genuine and real. "You always look good."

"Now you're the one being polite," she teased, her heart picking up speed.

"I've never been accused of that before."

"There's a first for everything."

"Yea, you scared the sh—stuffing out of me."

Suzanne laughed. "The stuffing?"

"I'm trying to be polite and remember you're a lady not used to raw language."

"I don't mind if you swear."

His teasing tone grew serious. "Because you expect it?"

"No, because most times I want to swear myself."

His gaze intensified. "I see."

Suzanne lowered her gaze, unable to look at him any longer, but it landed on his chest, which wasn't a safe place to look, especially when he smelled fresh from a shower. She watched a wayward drop of water flow down over his muscles and her fingers itched to do the same. If she moved just a little closer she could touch him and bask in the warmth of his body. She quickly lowered her gaze to her lap and gripped her hands. "Would you like something to drink?"

"I'd prefer something to eat."

"Oh." She stood and grabbed her handbag. She pretended to look at the money in her wallet, although there wasn't much there. "What are you in the mood for?"

He stood. "Let's see what's in your kitchen."

She stared at him alarmed. He wanted to eat *in?* "I'm not much of a cook."

"I bet you don't cook at all."

"I learned to cook some," she said defensively.

"I guess some things do change."

"A lot of things change."

"I know," he said with a sly smile, and then he walked into the kitchen. She followed him and saw him opening the cupboards.

He raised an eyebrow in disbelief at the bare items. "Is this how you keep your girlish figure? By starving yourself?"

"I haven't had a chance to shop." She didn't have the money, either, and preferred to stay out of town. "What are you doing here, anyway?" she asked, hoping to divert his attention.

Rick opened the fridge and shook his head in disgust by the lack of choices. "I came to look at the house again in a different light."

"Would you like me to show you around?"

He bent down to look farther into the fridge. "Let's eat first."

"I'm not hungry."

"I am." He straightened and turned to her with a pained expression. "Do you know how much lawn you have?"

She licked her lips, feeling guilty. "I'm really grateful. There's a deli—"

"We're eating here." He pulled out items from the fridge. "Set the table."

She blinked. "What?"

"You know how to set the table, right? Or do you usually have someone do that for you?"

She frowned. "Of course I can set a table. I learned at the age of three."

"I only learned last year. You think I'm kidding?" Rick said, noticing her smirk. "When we were ready for dinner at my house we just pulled back the plastic on the TV dinner."

Suzanne got the plates and utensils and placed them on the table. "That's a lie. Your mother knows how to cook. I tried out her oatmeal cookies at a bake sale."

"That's the only thing she knows how to make. That and a tequila sunrise."

"Then how did you learn to cook?" she asked as she watched the ease in which he moved about in the kitchen.

"Didn't have a choice. Fast food adds up and frozen dinners can start to taste the same. Besides, you wouldn't believe how much you can make with a can of beans and some rice."

"Oh, yes I remember when…" She stopped.

He turned to her. "You remember what?"

"You probably won't remember."

"I remember a lot of things," he said in a deep voice that stirred the hairs on the back of her neck. "Try me."

"It's nothing."

He stared at her for a long moment, then shrugged. "Fine."

She watched Rick cook. He looked remarkably comfortable in her kitchen, although he shouldn't have. She studied him as he moved, captivated by the symmetry of his body as his muscles constricted and relaxed with each motion. She saw the scar on his left shoulder and another on his right side and felt a twinge of pain as though they were new and fresh. She remembered when he'd told her about the first one in a low flat voice that chilled her, and she recalled how he'd gotten the second one. They'd both come from his father. She turned her gaze away and studied the plates. "I'm sorry what I said before about your father."

He shrugged. "I'd forgotten about it." He said the words with a studied nonchalance, but the ease of his shoulders told her that her apology meant something to him.

Minutes later he placed a bowl of basil tomato soup and a grilled cheese sandwich in front of her.

Suzanne stared at the food, amazed by what he'd been able to create with her meager grocery items. "You're a magician."

Rick sat down in front of her. "No. I just know how to make do."

She took a bite. "Delicious."

"Hmm."

Suzanne tried to start a conversation, but his monosyllabic answers forced her to stop. Chitchat was never a talent of his and part of her was glad. Empty conversations bored her so she didn't mind the silence and focused on her food. She hadn't eaten this well in days and planned to enjoy it. When they were through she offered to wash the dishes and he offered to dry. She didn't need his help, but sensed he didn't plan to leave, at least not yet.

"So you're really interested in buying the house?" she asked as she handed him a plate.

Rick sent her an odd look. "Yes." He dried the plate then set it down and rested his hands on the counter. "Either you don't believe me or you're so used to men lying to you that you *can't* believe me." His gaze searched hers. "Not all men are liars and I've never lied to you, have I?"

Suzanne cleared her throat and handed him a cup, hoping to break his gaze. "No."

He didn't take the cup from her. "Then why would I start now?"

"Right. I'm sorry. I just don't see you living here."

His jaw twitched. "Because it's too grand for me?"

"No, it's too ordinary."

He grasped the cup, his fingers brushing hers. "There's nothing wrong with ordinary."

"No, but now you're anything but."

He grinned. "I've changed." His grin slowly widened. "But I can see you don't believe that, either, and I'm not going to try and convince you."

She handed him the last item then dried her hands. "I can show you the house again if you want. I don't believe I showed you the attic last time."

Rick was silent for a moment, studying her in a way that made her feel vulnerable. She wondered what he saw, then he said, "Lead the way."

Suzanne showed him the house again. This time she included areas she hadn't bothered to point out before. She proudly showed him the window seat under the bay window in a little alcove off the kitchen, and the extra-large pantry in the basement. Her grandparents were survivors of the Depression, and out of habit, kept a stockpile of nonperishable food items that could feed an entire village. Rick was impressed with the music studio off her father's study and the guest bedroom, with its own bathroom and minikitchenette that her parents had planned on using as a mother-in-law apartment for her grandmother when she was alive. Suzanne saved the attic for last. It was her favorite spot because it had the best view and had always been a place of solace. "Mom used it as an alcove." She pointed to the window. "And just look at that view."

Rick ran his hand along a beam. "So this is it."

"What?"

"Where you came to hide. You said you had to practice up here, but you also used it as a place to get away." When she looked at him in surprise, he laughed. "I told you I had a good memory."

"Yes."

He picked up the violin case sitting in the corner. "Do you still play?"

She stiffened. "No."

"Why not?"

Suzanne shrugged, not wanting to explain. "So that's it. You've seen the entire house twice." She glanced around, not knowing what else to say and fully aware of how cramped the quarters were. The attic had seemed large when she was a child, but now it felt stiflingly small. Or perhaps Rick made every space seem small. Nervously she began to squeeze by him to head down the stairs. "I've shown you everything you wanted to see."

He blocked her path. "No, you haven't."

"I haven't?"

"No, because I want to see you stop avoiding my

touch. I want to see you stop pretending we're strangers and I want to see you remember this." He pulled her to him and kissed her. Suzanne wanted to struggle against him and resist, but she didn't. She let herself indulge in the wild, punishing sweetness of his lips, the hands that held her soft curves into his hard form and that was all he needed. He deepened the kiss and she felt her body become fire. That's when she knew she was in danger and pulled away.

Suzanne grinned and said in a shaky voice, "I knew you hadn't changed." She tried to make her voice light to lessen the impact of their kiss.

But his smoldering gaze wouldn't let her. "I have changed Suzanne," he said in a dark voice, "but you're too afraid to believe that."

"Why would I be afraid?"

He took a step toward her.

She held her hand out. "I know you're used to getting what you want especially from the fairer sex. But let me tell you one thing. All you're getting from me is the house."

"Is that a challenge?

"It's a warning."

He winked. "You should know me better than that. Warnings only make me try harder," he said then walked down the stairs and left.

Suzanne gazed out the attic window and watched Rick get into his car and drive away. She touched her fingers to her lips and remembered a time he'd ignored a warning....

Chapter 6

It had been an unusually cold June the summer Suzanne was eighteen and she and her father had another of their monthly shouting matches.

"You're going to do exactly what I tell you because that's the way things work around here," he said as he sat behind the massive desk in his study. He was a powerfully built man with deep-set eyes and features no one would call handsome. His well-designed study made him look respectable but she knew there was a streak of ruthlessness behind his polish.

She held up the piece of paper in her hand. "But I got accepted into college."

"Well, that's fine, but you're not going. What do you need college for when I've got your life already planned for you? College is for the poor and middle-class people who need a trade. You don't need a trade. I'm in a trade so I know what I'm talking about. My road was a rocky one, but yours will be smooth. If you were a boy, that'd be different, but you're lucky. You're always going to be taken care of. And I'm not wasting money so you can get some useless four year degree in music. You play that violin well, but you don't have what it takes to make it a career."

"Dad, you sound archaic—"

"Archaic?" He chuckled. "Do you know how many young women would want to be *you?*" He pointed out the window. "Do you know how many women envy you? They envy you, your house, your money and your status." He tapped his chest. "That's all because of me. Fortunately, you got your looks from your momma."

"I don't care about those things."

"You would care if you didn't have them."

"I'm going to be a musician."

He leaned back and rested his hands on the desk. "What's going on here? You never used to defy me this way. You used to be such a good girl."

Yes, she'd been a slave to obedience since the day she was born. Her family used to tease her that as a baby she wouldn't even cry without permission. All her life she was the good daughter and her mother's pride and joy. She'd had a brother who'd died at five months and her parents had been unable to conceive any more children after her so she became their focus.

All their hopes and dreams lay on her shoulders and she never wanted to disappoint them, but as the years passed it seemed that her obedience wasn't enough. It wasn't enough to get straight A's, to be head cheerleader or first violin. None of that mattered as long as she followed the rules—her father's rules and they became more demanding.

"I just want to learn more," she said in a quiet voice.

He rose to his feet and came from behind his desk. "Let me see that letter."

She handed it over to him with pride. "It's a great school and not many people can get in."

"Hmm." He took the paper, then tore it into strips.

"No," Suzanne cried reaching for it. "You have no right."

He crumbled the strips in his fist. "I'm your father. I have every right." He pointed a finger at her. "You're going to work with your aunt and learn how to be a hostess. Then you're going to marry Wallace Lyon. He's smart and he's from a good family and he'll go far."

"But I don't love him."

He laughed. "You don't have to. You only have to marry him."

"I'll run away."

"And live on what? You want to break your mother's heart, and my heart too? After all we've done for you?"

Suzanne wiped away a tear, wishing she had the courage to leave them, but knowing she didn't.

He softened his voice. "You'll have a good life. Now—" He paused when she left the room. "Where do you think you're going?" he shouted after her.

Suzanne grabbed her coat from the hall stand. "I'm leaving."

"And where do you plan to go?" Her father said, amused.

"I don't know, but I need to get away from you," she said, slamming the door on her father's laughter.

Suzanne drove around for an hour before stopping at her former music teacher's house. She needed someone to talk to, even if they couldn't change anything, and Melba Lowell was a good listener. Suzanne knocked on the door and seconds later Melba opened it. Her usually lovely highlighted brown hair hung limp around her face and her brown eyes looked nervous.

"Suzanne," she said in a strained whisper. "Now is not a good time."

Suzanne took a step back to leave but noticed the bruise on Melba's arm. "Do you need me to call the police?"

"I need you to go."

A loud belligerent voice called out her teacher's name. "Who's at the door?"

"A student." Melba chewed her lower lip. "Don't look like that Suzanne. He's just in one of his moods."

"Come with me," Suzanne said. "I've got my car."

"I can't."

"If I stay he can't touch you, right?" Suzanne was about to enter when she saw Melba's husband, Albert— a striking man of forty with silver hair and brownish-green eyes—standing behind her.

"Hello, Mr. Lowell."

His belligerent tone disappeared to one as sweet as pecan pie. "Hello, Suzanne."

"I came to talk to Miss Melba."

"She's busy right now."

"We all know what you do to her."

Melba reached out to Suzanne in a desperate gesture, stopped and clasped her hands together. "Suzanne, please."

He looked wounded. "I don't know what you're talking about. What a wild imagination you have. I know you like to make up stories." He rested a hand on Melba's shoulder. "Everyone knows how well I take care of my wife."

Suzanne couldn't ignore the possessive note in his tone. "One day everyone's going to know the truth."

"Suzanne," Melba said in a pleading tone. "Don't go spreading gossip. I just bumped into a table. That's all." She then mouthed, *Please go.*

Suzanne sighed. "I'll talk to you later."

"Maybe," Albert said, closing the door.

She was barely down the porch steps when she heard a glass shatter. A scream followed, then shouting. Suzanne stared at the house and started up the steps, but changed her mind. She tried to see through the windows, but the curtains were closed. She searched the quiet street trying to figure out what she should do. She didn't know what was going on, but she knew she had to do something. Suddenly she saw a man come out of one of the houses and race across the street. She halted when she saw who it was—Rick Gordon.

He stared at her, startled. "What's wrong?"

Her throat began to close. She'd never spoken more than two words to him her entire life and had always kept a proper distance. But now he was the only person she could turn to.

"You've got her all tongue-tied," his companion said. She hadn't noticed him before. He stood behind the truck.

"Shut up," Rick said. He took her by the shoulders and softened his voice. "What's wrong?"

It wasn't his voice or his hands that comforted her, it was his eyes. She could trust him.

"You have to help me," she said in a rush. "Call the police. He's at it again."

"Who?"

"Mr. Lowell. I shouldn't have stopped by. This is all my fault. He's hurting her."

Rick swore then turned to his workmate and said, "Call the police."

"They're not going to listen to me."

"Just call them," he said then raced across the street to the house, with Suzanne following him. He burst down the door and ran inside. "Miss Melba?"

Albert emerged from the kitchen like an enraged bear. "What the hell are you doing in my house, boy?"

"I heard a scream."

"You heard wrong." He looked past Rick and glared at Suzanne. "You've been telling stories again, haven't you?"

Rick moved in front of her, blocking Albert's view, and kept his voice low. "I just wanted to make sure that Miss Melba is all right."

"She's fine."

"I'd still like to see—"

Mr. Lowell took a threatening step toward him. "Are you calling me a liar?"

"No, sir."

"You owe me a new door."

"Yes, sir."

"How are you going to pay for it?"

"I have some money."

"Not much I bet."

"I'll save."

He folded his arms, tucking his anger behind a cool mask. "How long has your father been working for me? He wouldn't be too happy if he lost his job, would he?"

Suzanne trembled, realizing the impact of Mr. Lowell's threat. Everyone knew Rick's father was a mean drunk; he'd be even meaner without a job.

Rick kept his voice steady. "As I said, we heard a scream."

Melba peeked her head out. "I just lost my balance and was startled. It's okay."

The sound of sirens suddenly pierced the air. Albert swore and pointed a finger at Suzanne. "This is all your fault. You're trying to cause trouble."

"I called the police," Rick said.

Mr. Lowell grinned. "Trying to make good with the judge's daughter?"

When the police arrived, Mr. Lowell briefed them on the situation, providing them with his story. Melba readily agreed. They apologized and hurried out. One of the officers—a female with spiky black hair who looked like she could hammer nails with her fist—took Rick aside. "I should have known you'd be behind this."

Suzanne spoke up. "He called because of me."

The officer ignored her. "I know the ladies like you, but this isn't your kind of neighborhood."

"I was on a job," Rick said.

"What kind of job?" the officer asked snidely, referring to his brother who was in jail for burglary.

"I was working over there." He pointed to the house across the street.

"I was the one who wanted to call," Suzanne insisted. "I thought something was wrong."

At last the officer noticed her and smiled. "Everything is okay. I know you were trying to help, but your father would have a heart attack if he saw who you were with. You're a good girl and I hope you plan to stay that way." She sent Rick an ugly look. "Go home." She shifted her gaze to Suzanne. "Both of you." She got back into her patrol car and started it.

Rick didn't move. He watched the car drive away, his face a mask of anger and Suzanne felt the injustice of it all. Mr. Lowell was the villain, but everyone treated Rick as though he were. She knew from his reputation that he wasn't a saint, but the officer's treatment didn't sit well with her. He had come to the rescue and had been reprimanded instead of thanked. Suddenly, her mother's words came to her: "A sweet word can turn away anger." He needed kindness. He needed E.T.W.

Suzanne swallowed, her heart racing, she took a deep breath before staring up at him. "Rick?"

He shifted his dark gaze to her face and she briefly lost courage, but she didn't look way. She touched his arm in a soft fleeting gesture. "You're one of the bravest men I've ever known. Thank you for helping me." She smiled, but he didn't return the expression. She let her shoulders sag in defeat. "Goodbye." She walked to her car.

"Don't thank me," he said in a soft voice. "I didn't do anything."

She turned to him. "Yes, you did."

He shook his head. "No, I didn't. She didn't press charges. Do you know why?"

"No, she should have." Suzanne leaned against her car and stared at the Lowell house in disbelief. "They would have taken him away."

"She's afraid."

"Of what?"

"That he'll get out and hurt her some more."

"Then she should leave him."

Rick shook his head, amused by her naiveté. "Things must be nice and neat in your own little world."

"He's a bad man."

"He's also a powerful man."

"But there are laws."

"There are ways to get around the law." Rick stared at her. "Don't mess with him. I don't care who your father is."

Her father. The image of him suddenly loomed large in her thoughts and forced her to remember their argument earlier that evening, which reared fresh in her mind like a monster. She thought of how her father ruled her life and then she thought of poor Melba having to succumb to her husband. A feeling of helplessness enveloped her and she leaned against her car and tears slid down her face.

Rick made his voice gentle and rested an arm on her shoulder. "Hey, what's this?" He reached to touch her face but stopped himself, clenching his hand into a fist. "Don't do that."

"Why not? You're right. We didn't do anything. Nothing's changed. Nothing will ever change."

"That's not true."

She sniffed. "What?"

"We can change. I'm not going to live like this

forever. I've got dreams and one day I'll leave this town and come back and everyone will respect me. Even—" He bit his lip then took out a rag from his back pocket. "Wipe your eyes."

She held the rag, unsure.

"It's clean."

"It's not that. It smells like licorice."

A brief smile touched his lips. "I admit, I'm an addict. Want some?"

She dabbed her eyes. "No, thank you."

"You don't have to be that polite about it."

She laughed. "I can't help it."

"Hmm." He rested a hand against the hood of her car.

Soon the tears stopped and she stared at him. She didn't see the boy with the wild reputation who was wearing a shirt so faded that the words couldn't be read anymore, who looked so poor. Instead she saw a young man who had come to her aid and Melba's aid, too. He wasn't like her father or Mr. Lowell. He was different. He was everything her father told her to stay away from—he was mysterious, dangerous, tempting and her father wasn't there. He couldn't tell her what to do now.

"I'd better go," he said, taking a step back.

"I meant what I said before. You're the bravest man I've ever known. You're the type of man songs are written about. The kind of man who braves the battlefields, who tames the wilderness and conquers new lands. You're everything women admire about men."

He took another step back. "Uh…you were just afraid."

She took a step forward. "No, with you I could never be afraid." She clasped his hand and placed the rag in it. "Somehow *thank you* doesn't seem enough."

He glanced down at her hand then slowly met her gaze. "It is," he said in a raw husky voice.

His eyes clung to hers and neither moved. They didn't dare. They knew the risk was great, but so was the temptation. Neither could remember who moved first, but the moment their lips touched they didn't regret it for a second. To Suzanne, his lips were wet, warm and incredibly sweet. The impact of their kiss surprised them both, but they didn't pull away. She wrapped her arms around his neck and drew him closer, but he drew away and said, "Give me your keys."

"What?"

He held out his hand with impatience. "Just do it."

She did and he opened the door and got into the driver's seat of her red Mustang. "Get in."

Suzanne followed his order, filled with questions. "What about your partner?"

"He knows how to get home."

"What about you?"

"We'll discuss that later." And that was the last thing he said as he sped down the street. Minutes later he drove into a remote spot near the edge of town and turned off the engine and turned to her. "Now no one can see us."

"Okay."

"Do you know what you're doing?"

"Yes."

"I'm not sure you do. You're taking a risk getting involved with me."

"I know that, too."

He lowered his voice and gently caressed her cheek. "Do you know how much?"

She rested a hand on his thigh. "As long as no one knows, how much trouble could that be?"

He smiled. "So the judge's perfect daughter has a rebellious side."

"You'll find out if you kiss me again."

He did. More than once. And they went from the front seat into the backseat and that began their summer affair.

If only it had ended as innocently as it had started.

If only it had remained sneaking out at night and lovemaking in the backseat of a car. But somehow it had become more. She'd played her violin for him and he had shown her some of his inventions and the sketches for other ideas he had. They talked about their families and occasionally about the future.

For several weeks she'd allowed herself to believe that Rick had come to care for her as she had for him and perhaps things would have turned out different if Melba hadn't blown her husband away with a shotgun.

Chapter 7

The incident divided the community along economic lines overnight. Mr. Lowell was a solid citizen who'd married beneath him. Many believed if things had been so bad his wife could have left; instead she'd turned to murder. When Melba was indicted, the first person Suzanne wanted to see was Rick so they set up a meeting place—the old red barn on one of the properties the Fulfords were trying to sell.

Suzanne arrived first and waited. When she heard footsteps she turned around.

"He's not coming," her father said with a cold smile.

Goose bumps scurried up her arms. "What do you mean?" she said, shocked to see her father standing there.

"Don't play coy with me. I know what you've been up to these last couple of months and that's fine. Just like young men sow their oats before they settle down, every young woman should have a chance to become experienced, too, before she marries. But summer's almost over and that time is up."

"Dad—"

"This trial is going to be dirty and I would hate it to spill over in unnecessary ways. I know that Rick used to go by a lot of young ladies' houses, if you want to call them that. You know he's very familiar with the ladies."

"He's been with me," Suzanne replied defiantly, wanting and hoping to hurt him.

"No one's to know that and if there were witnesses who saw him with Melba…" He let his words trail off, making his meaning clear. Witnesses would appear if he wanted them to. "He already has a bleak future. I'd hate to see it go any lower. Wouldn't you?"

"Melba killed her husband in self-defense and Rick had nothing to do with it."

Her father nodded. "Yes, that can be the story you tell once you're engaged."

"What did you say to him?"

"I just let him know that you changed your mind. I didn't lie, did I?"

"I'm not giving him up."

"He's not worth keeping. You'd get better use from an old dishrag than to saddle yourself with a Gordon. I've known about them longer than you. They're all bad. You've had your fun and now it's over. You don't want to fight me, Suzanne. I always win and I know what's best for you."

"You think you know what's best for everyone."

"That's my job and I'm usually right."

Suzanne spun away, knowing she couldn't beat him. He was always right because he made sure things worked out in his favor. She drove home wondering what she could do next. Three times she drove to Rick's house, but every time either his father or mother answered and closed the door in her face. Calling him wasn't any better. Then one day she saw him coming out of Goodwin's Hardware store. She called out his name before he got into his truck.

"Whatever my father said wasn't true," she said once she'd reached him.

"So you still want to see me?" he asked with a guarded look.

Yes. "I can't."

"So what part wasn't true?"

"The reason why."

He tossed his purchases inside the truck. "You don't have to explain yourself, I understand," he declared with cool detachment. "No big deal. We were just having fun."

Each word fell on her heart like boulders. "Right."

A pretty young woman in a bright pink dress that made Suzanne look as though she was wearing a burlap bag, came up to him and whispered something in his ear. Her name was Hannah Fulford and she was Della's second cousin. Her family owned two stores and she was allowed more liberties than the other girls in Anadale because her father was dead and her mother couldn't control her.

Rick smiled in response to her words, patted her on the butt and said, "See you tonight."

Hannah glanced at Suzanne. "No need to worry

about me, Suzanne, no one else does." She grinned and turned as Rick watched her saunter away. He looked at Suzanne with a bored expression. "As you can see I'm not heartbroken."

"Right," she said again, her mouth dry. It was all she could say. If she said any more she was afraid she'd cry and embarrass herself. He'd moved on. She meant nothing to him. She'd been just another notch on his belt. She'd been foolish to expect more.

"I know I won't get an invitation, but I know you'll make a beautiful bride." He got into his truck and closed the door. "Goodbye, Suzanne."

"Goodbye." She watched him drive off, letting the dust mingle with her tears.

That year Melba was convicted of murder and the year after Suzanne became Mrs. Wallace Lyon. She rarely saw Rick before he moved away. Years later, after a loveless and childless marriage, Suzanne divorced and left town. But now she and Rick were back in Anadale.

But she knew she wasn't back to stay. And she wouldn't be hurt again. Suzanne turned from the attic window, wishing she could block out her memories. The next day roses arrived from Wallace, after that Belgian chocolates. He sent a different item every day for the entire week. She kept the gifts because she knew returning them would only make him more determined. She didn't know why he wanted her back, but didn't care. A week later she received the call she'd been hoping for.

"He made an offer on the house," Della told Suzanne over the phone.

"Who?"

"Rick. He'll buy it at the asking price."

Suzanne sank into her chair, relieved. "Wonderful, tell him I accept." Now she'd be free to leave town and start over.

"Great," Della squeaked. "Toodles."

On the day of the signing, Suzanne wore her most stylish outfit and a broad-rimmed white hat. At last the burden of the house and her father's debts would be over. When she entered the office building and saw Rick sitting on a bench in the hallway, Suzanne did a double take. She couldn't believe the gorgeous man in the business suit was the same one who'd mowed her lawn over a week ago. He looked like a worldly stranger and his suit seemed to hide all that she knew he was. Then she saw an attractive woman pass by him and also give him a second look, which he returned in kind. The woman blushed and hurried off. Rick grinned at her. At that moment, Suzanne knew no suit could completely hide his character. When it came to women, Rick was a wolf, just like the rest of them.

He stood up when he saw her. "Hello."

"Hello." Suzanne took off her hat and looked at the office door. "Why are you waiting outside? Is something wrong?"

"No, I was waiting for you."

"Oh." She didn't know what else to say so she knocked on the door to the lawyer's office. A petite, perky young woman, wearing a tie-dye sundress and a pair of four-inch killer high heels, opened the door and invited them to enter. She led them into a small conference room. Suzanne set her hat on the table and sat. "Della better not be late for this."

Rick sat beside her. "Don't worry, I saw her in the hall, she'll be right back."

"Good."

They turned when they heard the door open, but instead of Della there was the woman from the hallway. She leaned over Rick and whispered something in his ear then slipped a piece of paper in his hand before leaving. Rick absently shoved the note in his jacket pocket.

"Aren't you going to read it?" Suzanne asked.

He rested his arms on the table and grinned. "I already know what it says."

"Of course." Probably a phone number with the words *Call me.*

He reached into his pocket. "Would you like to see?"

"No," she said too quickly.

He shrugged. "You seemed interested."

"I'm not interested. Just curious."

"Hmm. Two words that mean the same thing."

Suzanne began to argue, but at that moment Della returned with the lawyer responsible for the closing, and they got down to business. Suzanne barely looked at the stack of documents before signing them. She wrote her name with the same flourish as she signed her books. She pushed the papers over to Rick and watched him sign. She didn't know she was holding her breath until he set his pen down. At last it was over. The house was now his. Her problems were over.

She didn't know who handed her the cashier's check, she just remembered the feel of the paper in her hand and all that it represented.

"How about lunch?" Rick asked.

Suzanne glanced up and saw him standing beside her. She folded up the check and put it in her purse. "I can't. I have errands."

He leaned against the table, looking every bit the wealthy man he was—handsome, debonair, inviting. "I guess it doesn't help, huh?"

She stared up at him unsure. "What?"

"My money. You still don't want to be seen with me in public."

Suzanne stood and put on her hat. "That's not true."

"It was true at one time."

"And you don't want me to forget that, do you?"

"I'm asking you to lunch."

Suzanne headed for the door. "Another time."

He followed her. "I doubt there will be one," he scoffed. "How long are you planning to stick around?"

"A few weeks," she said, wishing he would leave her alone. "I have thirty days to get things packed up and get out of the house."

"So you won't be sneaking out of town soon?"

"I don't sneak."

He shoved a hand in his pocket. "You're sure you don't want lunch?"

"I'm sure."

"Even if it's just an hour?"

"Yes."

"I hate eating alone."

She stopped and stared at him. "Then find someone else, you always could." She started to walk away.

He stepped in front of her. "How about dinner?"

"No." She moved to the side.

He blocked her again. "Breakfast?"

"Definitely not." When he blocked her path again she threw up her hands, aggravated. "Why would you want to eat with me?"

"I had fun last time. I know you did, too."

She rested a hand on her hip.

"Do you deny it?"

"We hardly said anything."

"It's possible to be with someone and not say a word."

She rested her other hand on her hip fully understanding his sexual overtone. Although heat flooded her cheeks she refused to be intimidated. "Listen. I'm no longer a virgin filled with lust. Promises, tokens and a suggestion of a 'good time' can no longer seduce me. Men can use those well worn methods to lead other women into misery, but I've traveled that path before and I've chosen another direction. I suggest you put that phone number to good use and leave me alone."

"I'm glad you still know about it."

"What?"

"Lust."

She widened her eyes. "I didn't say—"

He loosened his tie. "You didn't have to say anything. I can read your eyes." He leaned toward her. "And your eyes don't lie." He held her gaze. "How about lunch tomorrow?"

"Then you'll leave me alone?"

"I thought you didn't like promises."

She briefly closed her eyes and let out a fierce sigh. "Fine, I'll see you tomorrow."

"Great. I'll pick you up."

Suzanne watched him leave, his cocky walk making it clear that the wolf was on the prowl, but she was determined that she wouldn't be his prey.

"Goodness, he's even better from this angle," Della said behind her.

"And he knows it," Suzanne grumbled. "I'm just glad that's all over. The house is sold." She remembered the check in her purse, said goodbye to Della and raced to her car. Once inside, she pulled out her cell phone and called their family lawyer, Mrs. Maloney, and told her about the house sale.

"At least that's something," she said.

Suzanne paused, stunned by her lack of enthusiasm. "What do you mean 'that's something'? I thought you wanted me to sell the house."

"I did, but that will only cover the mortgages. Let me remind you of your father's other debts," Mrs. Maloney said and started to read a list. By the tenth item Suzanne groaned and shut her eyes.

"Okay," she said, resigned. "I get it. I'm not out of the woods yet."

"Honey, you're not even out of the forest."

She rubbed her temple. "What am I going to do?"

"I've been to the house. You have some very nice furnishings and I know an antiques dealer who could get them sold at an excellent price."

"An auction?" Suzanne said, appalled. "I can't have the town know that I'm selling my family heirlooms."

"We'll conduct a discreet auction. It will be out of town. Just you leave things to me. I'll have my man stop by tomorrow."

"Right," Suzanne said in a flat voice. "Could he come in the morning? I have a lunch—uh…meeting."

"Say ten?"

"That will work. Thank you."

"Suzanne, things will work out."

"Hmm," she said, wanting to believe her.

At home Suzanne looked at all her family possessions with a sinking sensation that threatened to choke her. There was the decorative, ornate writing desk in her father's study that reminded her of the few fun times she spent pretending to be her father's secretary when she was a child. In the hallway sat an antique Chinese vase, which was used as an umbrella stand. But the one item she knew she would miss the most was the large mahogany coatrack her great-great-grandfather had made by hand. It was considered a family heirloom and Suzanne felt a surge of sadness, knowing that now money had become more important than memories. Her heart ached and she felt a lump in her throat, but she was determined not to cry.

The next day Suzanne flipped through the few items in her closet wondering what she should wear for her meeting with Rick. She'd given most of her wardrobe to a consignment shop for money. She finally selected a light blue silk pantsuit. She ate a quick breakfast, but barely had a chance to finish when she heard the antiques dealer drive up. She dumped her dishes in the sink and ran to the front door. She opened it before he could knock.

He was a short man with long blond hair and a mustache. They briefly chatted, and then he went quickly through several rooms, ending in the living room. She silently watched him and after a few minutes he shook his head and let out a weary sigh. "I'm sorry, Ms. Rand," he said as they stood in the foyer.

"Why?"

"They're all fakes."

She laughed, certain he was joking. "They can't be."

His mustache twitched with dismay. "They are. Here, let me show you." He took the two battered umbrellas out of the Chinese vase and turned it upside down.

"Do you see what is written here?" He beckoned for Suzanne to take a closer look. The wording said "Made in China." Then he showed her what was wrong with the old grandfather clock that sat on the mantle in the living room, it had remade parts that were clearly made in the twentieth century. Next he showed her that the dining room table and chairs were not totally made of wood, but had veneered Formica inserted in the joints.

The most disappointing of all was the fact that the freestanding armoire in the master bedroom was simply an excellent replica of old English woodwork and the hardware was not "old" anything, but rather recent salvaged parts.

She stopped him before he could continue anymore. "Enough. I've heard enough."

"I'm very sorry."

"I don't understand. My mother's family had these antiques appraised and insured them."

"Then someone must have sold the real ones and replaced them with reproductions. They're excellent replicas."

She sank against the wall. "So I don't have anything of value?"

"You could still do a sale, but you won't get as much as you'd hoped."

Suzanne covered her eyes. "I don't believe this."

"I'm sorry. I could look around some more."

"Maybe another time," Suzanne said, feeling tired. "I'll call you."

She led the dealer to the door and sat on the porch swing, staring at the lawn. Her father was a bigger bastard than she'd thought and she was in deeper financial trouble than she'd imagined. She didn't know how long she sat there. She saw the bright red wings of a cardinal as he darted through the sky, a gray squirrel scurry through the lawn and dash up a tree, and soon she saw Rick's black BMW drive up. She took a deep breath to steady herself. She'd eat lunch with him then come home and bury herself under the covers.

He stopped at the foot of the porch steps and stared up at her. "What's wrong?"

"Nothing," she said, surprised by his question. She looked at the bag in his hand. "Is that lunch?"

He nodded.

"Good, it's a nice day. Why don't we have a picnic? I'll get a blanket and dishes." She didn't give him a chance to argue. She didn't want to be inside the house of lies with him any longer than she had to. When she reemerged he was still standing in the same spot. He sent her an odd look, but didn't say anything.

"How about near the magnolia tree over there?" she said and started to walk down the stairs.

He stepped in front of her. "No."

She halted, startled. "What?"

"What's going on?"

"I told you it's nothing."

"You're lying to me," he said in a low voice that made her take a step back.

She turned to the door. "If you'd prefer to eat inside—"

"You had that same look on your face that night." He rested his hands on her shoulder and slowly turned her around. "You trusted me before, why won't you trust me now?" He took the plates and blanket from her and set them on the porch swing then cradled her face. "Wasn't I there for you?"

Suzanne squeezed her eyes shut, feeling herself weaken under his touch. His hands were as she remembered and their tenderness made her tremble. She couldn't deny how vulnerable his touch made her feel, how the sensation of his hands went through her.

"Yes," she said in an anguished whisper. She took his wrists and removed his hands from her face. "But you walked away."

"You wanted me to."

Because I couldn't make you stay. "I don't want to talk about the past."

"Are you going to ask me what I'm doing here?"

"To have lunch."

"You don't suspect that there's another reason?"

Suddenly everything about him became clear. He wasn't the man in the suit, or the one in the work clothes. He wasn't just a handyman or a millionaire. He was something different and he was no longer a stranger. She knew him. She knew that he liked black licorice and listening to bluegrass. That he hated the sight of lightning but loved the sound of thunder. All those dormant feelings came rushing back like an avalanche and again there was no father to stop her.

Just as she had done that night all those years ago, she threw away her inhibitions and surrendered to her feelings. "I do," she said, placing her lips on his.

Chapter 8

She tasted even better the second time, Rick thought as Suzanne's soft lips welcomed his onslaught. His plan had been to wait until after the picnic for this moment, but he always seized an opportunity that presented itself. But something was different with this kiss from that one in the attic. This one was too close to the first kiss they'd had. The one that had changed everything for him and he would never let that happen again. He was the master seducer, but he had to make sure he wasn't the one being seduced.

He went still then drew away from her. It took all his effort to do so because at that moment his body was tense and hot and he wanted nothing more than to seek release between her thighs, but he wasn't going to be used again. He wasn't going to relinquish his control.

When she was in his arms again it would be because she wanted *him*. Not just because he was handy and useful. He wasn't going to repeat the past. One day Suzanne would be his completely, but today wasn't that day. He spun away from her and gripped the porch railing.

"What's wrong?" Suzanne asked. He could hear the worry in her voice. He was glad she was worried, she needed to be.

He took a deep steadying breath to compose himself before meeting her eyes. "That's what I asked you." He raised his hand when she opened her mouth. "And don't waste your time lying to me."

Suzanne smiled and leaned forward, giving him a tantalizing view of her cleavage. "I didn't realize you were that interested in my problems."

He forced himself not to notice the invitation as a bead of sweat slid down his back. "So you admit that you have some?"

Her smile dimmed and this time worry entered her eyes instead of her voice. Her weakness was his advantage and he regained control. "Do I need to ask you again?"

"Let's eat first." She scooped up the blanket, plates and utensils and went inside. He grabbed the bag and followed. He sat at the table and watched her spread things out—each movement deliberate and swift. She wasn't upset or angry. She was furious and that made him only want her more. Her anger made her more human. He loved seeing the fire flow through those ice veins of hers. However, she was back on her pedestal, but he wouldn't let that last long. He knew that one day she'd be knocked off that high perch and would fall into the gutter where she thought he belonged. Now they were equals and one day she'd have to admit it. Suzanne finally sat down at the table and fixed her plate. She ate as though she were dining at a high-priced restaurant in downtown Durham. Rick watched her for a few minutes. "So why did you come back here?"

"You know why," she replied with cool politeness.

Rick shook his head. "At first I thought your kitchen was bare because you didn't plan to stay long, but then I began to wonder why you came back at all."

"I'm taking care of things. You know that."

"You could have had someone else sell the house for you. Isn't that what your family always did? It's what you're used to. Why didn't you hire someone to mow or keep the garden up? Tell me the truth."

Suzanne gripped her fork before slowly setting it down and clasping her hands together. "I think you already know the truth."

"I just want to make sure."

"You mean you want me to admit it."

"Yes."

Suzanne pushed herself from the table and folded her arms, staring at Rick like they were adversaries at war. "Oh, I see. Your moment of triumph has arrived. This is what you wanted. You weren't just after the house or even me," she said with a bitter laugh. "You wanted to hear me admit my ruin."

Something cold touched his heart as if something fragile but beautiful between them had died. It wasn't her words that caused regret to assail him, it was her face. Her expression, that devastating look of betrayal and helplessness. She could mask it from others with her tightly schooled features, but he'd always been able to see it in her eyes. He'd seen it before, but had never been the cause of it. "No that's not—"

She shoved herself from the table. "Don't disappoint me, Rick. You promised not to lie to me. I'm used to men lying remember? I thought you were different." She lifted her glass and took a delicate sip. "So what would you like me to admit first?"

"Look, I didn't mean—"

She took another sip. "My father left me a whole lot of debt, which is why I had to sell the house. Now why didn't I just hire someone to sell it for me? Because I'm broke. I lost my money to bad investments and my agent ran off with the rest. I haven't written anything in three years because I've already proven to be a failure and don't want to be again. Does that confession suit you? Are you ready to gloat?" She lifted her glass. "Let's make a toast to the fall of the mighty Rands."

"Suzanne, I—"

"I don't need your pity. I'm just telling you the truth. I know you hated my father and never cared much for me." She laughed with cruel irony. "You didn't even want pity sex, that says a lot."

Rick leaned forward, desperate for her to understand. "That's not why I stopped kiss—"

She ignored him and slammed the glass down on the table. "You're going to love this. I'd hoped the sale of the house would have fixed all my problems, but now I have to sell the furniture, too. But guess what?" She waited. "Don't you want to guess?"

"No, I—"

"Everything is basically worthless. Dad sold all the genuine pieces so there goes my chance of an auction."

"I can buy the furniture."

"I'm sure you can buy a lot of things."

"I'm offering to help you."

She shook her head. "It won't be enough."

"Tell me how much you need."

"No."

"You don't want to be in my debt?"

"No, I don't want to make you pay antique prices for cheap reproductions. I may not have money, but I still have my pride and integrity."

"I wouldn't know the difference."

She frowned. "Between pride and integrity?"

"No, the fakes from the originals."

"I would. But thanks for your charitable offer, Mr. Gordon."

He frowned at her use of his name. "Don't start that."

"I'm giving you respect, Mr. Gordon. Isn't that what you want? Isn't that what you're paying for?"

Rick came around the table and seized her shoulders. "Suzanne, stop it."

"I thought you liked stories."

He tightened his grip. "I said stop it."

"Stop what?" she shot back. "Stop telling you the truth? Isn't that what you wanted?"

"You've got it all wrong." He reached to touch her face, but she jerked away from him and he let his hand fall. "I didn't come here to—" He swore when his cell phone rang. He looked at the number before swearing again. "I have to take this, just give me a second. Sit down and eat something."

"I'm not—"

"Sit down anyway," he snapped and answered his phone. "Hi, honey," he said then left the room.

Suzanne didn't move. Not because she couldn't but because she was ashamed. She'd noticed the change in Rick's tone when he'd responded to the voice on the phone and watched as he gripped his hands into fists. Of course he'd have to stop their conversation for a woman. He was never without one. And she'd nearly made herself another bauble on his long chain—again. How dumb could she be? The last kiss in the attic had been on his terms just the way he liked it—swift, hot and simple. He'd done it to prove a point. This time she'd gotten the message—she didn't matter. She was glad she'd told him everything. At least she didn't have to pretend anymore.

Rick returned, looking grim. "I have to go."

"Okay," she said in a hollow tone. "Thank you for lunch."

"If I had more time—"

"But you don't so goodbye."

He hesitated. "Do you mind if I bring someone by tomorrow? I want them to see the house."

Suzanne stood and began clearing the table. "It's your house, Mr. Gordon. You don't have to ask permission."

He glanced up at the ceiling. "Don't do this."

"Do what? I'm giving you the respect you deserve. What you've always craved. You've gotten all that you've wanted and you came back to town because you're rich and I'm poor. You're a success and I'm a failure. I don't care if you pity me, but don't pretend to care."

"Suzanne," he said, his voice a plea. "That's not—" He stopped and swore when his phone rang again.

"Must be nice to be so popular." She set the dishes in the sink.

He looked at the number then put the phone away. "We'll talk about the furniture later."

She turned the faucet on full blast. "There's nothing to talk about."

He turned the faucet off. "I'll see you tomorrow around eleven."

"Whatever suits you, Mr. Gordon."

He stared at her as though he wanted to say more and she boldly stared back, daring him to. He pounded his fist against the counter and left.

Suzanne stood and waited for the front door to close and the moment it did, she sank into a chair, rested her head in her arms and began to sob.

Chapter 9

That night Suzanne slept in the attic. She moved aside some of her old things stored there and pulled out an old futon. The attic was the one place that didn't remind her of her father's influence. As she looked around the small space she thought about the apartment she'd rented right after her divorce. It was the first time she'd lived alone and she'd felt inadequate. At that time she didn't know how to balance a checkbook, pay bills or cook. She'd depended on Wallace and their chef for so much. Growing up she'd watched her housekeeper, Neena, in the kitchen, but had never participated in preparing a meal. Years later she'd been forced to learn how.

Suzanne sat on the futon fighting a returning feeling of inadequacy. She'd been down before but she was eager to rally again. She'd written one book. She could write another. And if it failed she didn't care. At least she would have tried. It was better than living with the constant fear that had haunted her these past years, a fear that her first book had been a fluke. A lucky break. She feared she wasn't good enough. All the men in her life thought she wasn't good enough, but she was determined that Rick would be the last man to make her feel that way. She'd prove to him—to all of them—that she was strong and worthy. That she could not be broken. That she wasn't the simpering belle her mother used to be or the society maven her aunt Bertha tried to make her. Then she remembered a statement her aunt always repeated: "You can either be a weeping willow or a magnolia." Suzanne thought of the strength and beauty of a magnolia tree and made a decision. She would be just as majestic and sturdy.

Soon the first line of a story came to mind. She grabbed her laptop and began to write in a hot creative rush. She based the story on another character from her fictional town of Waverly. One who needed redemption and in her book she would offer it to him. Time blurred into nothingness as she filled the computer screen with words, using language to paint pictures and sketch scenes. Suzanne didn't notice that the sun had set until she decided to take a minibreak to stretch her back and fingers. She yawned then looked at her watch—it was two o'clock in the morning.

She had to get some sleep before her visitors arrived. Suzanne drifted off to sleep with a sense of renewal. Although she was financially poor, she was still a Rand and proud to be one. Rick may be rich now, but she was

Suzanne Rand bestselling author and she felt she was on the verge of another blockbuster.

The loud "teakettle-teakettle" call of a Carolina wren greeting the morning woke her from her brief sleep. She showered and changed into an old shirt and jeans. She didn't see the point in dressing up for her guests. There was nothing to prove anymore. No facade to maintain. She didn't look like the frump she'd become after marrying Wallace, but no one would recognize her as Suzanne Rand the successful novelist and she didn't care. She didn't mind fading into the background, the house was all that mattered.

She ate a light breakfast of toast with scrambled eggs and orange juice, and went into her father's study to continue working on her story. She was busy drafting a major scene when she heard Rick's car pull into the driveway. She reluctantly set her laptop aside and went to greet them.

When she opened the door the first thing she noticed was Rick's expression. He didn't smile, however the woman next to him did—broadly. "Sorry, we're late," she said.

"No, you're right on time," Suzanne said, trying to mask her surprise. The woman wasn't anything she'd expected. She was lovely, in a wholesome way, from her outmoded dress to her overly pressed hair. Suzanne could feel Rick's gaze on her, but fought to combat any effect he had on her. He would not make her melt or tingle or feel uneasy. He wouldn't make her feel anything. She was numb and she would not let him penetrate her shield again.

"I'm Mandy and this is Luke," the woman said, glancing down.

Suzanne followed her gaze and noticed a little toffee-colored boy of about five wearing a large baseball cap with a picture of a frog on it. She gaped at him. Rick was with a woman who had a son? She quickly recovered herself. "It's a pleasure to meet you both," she stammered.

"You, too," Mandy said, and then she nudged the boy.

He slowly raised his head and said in a soft voice, "A pleasure, ma'am," as though he'd practiced it many times.

Suzanne stared at him, frozen with astonishment. He looked exactly like Rick. He had a perfectly shaped head, with finely cropped black-brown hair, large dark eyes surrounded by sweeping lashes that any woman would envy; he also had a small, perfectly shaped nose and rosebud lips, the color of pink taffy. He was beautiful and soon the image before her became clear. This wasn't just some woman with a child. This was *his* child.

Suzanne looked at Mandy's hand and didn't see a ring, but was sure that would come soon enough. She glanced at the porch swing and the embarrassment of her behavior yesterday rushed back to her with painful clarity. Like her father and Wallace, Rick probably liked his women on the side to be docile and unobtrusive. Instantly she realized that she'd asked for something she knew he could never give—loyalty and faithfulness.

Suzanne stepped back and opened the door wider. "Please do come in. The house is yours. No place is off-limits."

"It's not what you think," Rick said in a low voice, glancing at Mandy who was sniffing the freshly picked flowers in the foyer.

"How do you know what I'm thinking?" Suzanne replied in a cool tone, not meeting his gaze. "Are you a mind reader?"

He stepped in front of her. "I can explain."

She turned away and straightened a picture on the wall. "There's no need to."

"I won't show them your bedroom."

"You can show them any room you want to. I'm staying in the attic." She smiled at him with smug indifference. "Don't worry, I don't plan to stay long, Mr. Gordon."

"Call me Mr. Gordon one more time and you will regret it," he said in an acid tone.

"That won't be anything new. I regret a lot of things when it comes to you."

His jaw twitched, but before he could say anything, Mandy called out to him from the living room.

"Oh, it's beautiful," she said, darting through the rooms like a kid in a toy shop. "Rick it's wonderful. Has your mother seen it yet?"

"Not yet, but soon."

"And the furniture is perfect." She rushed over to an item on the mantle. "Wow, a genuine antique clock."

Suzanne shook her head. "Actually, it's—"

Rick rested a hand on her shoulder and gave it a slight squeeze. "Yes," he cut in.

"I'm surprised." Mandy looked at Suzanne. "You should see his apartment. Nothing in it is older than the last decade." Mandy smiled and studied the bookshelves.

Suzanne glared at him. "What are you up to? Or do you regularly lie to her?"

He grinned. "So you *are* interested in our relationship. You had me worried."

"I don't like deception."

He shrugged. "No one needs to know," he said, removing his hand.

Mandy looked at the dining room. "Rick, come see this."

He turned to Suzanne and said, "Don't leave," before following Mandy into the other room.

Suzanne was about to do just that when she noticed a small figure standing near the doorway. Luke. She'd forgotten about him. Had they forgotten him, too? Mandy was an absentminded mother if that was the case. The boy stared at the floor as if it were the most fascinating thing in the world. Suzanne loved children and had always hoped to have a few of her own, but fate hadn't given her that choice. She wondered if Rick knew how lucky he was.

She squatted in front of the boy. "My name is Miss Suzanne."

"Yes, ma'am," he said in the same soft tone as before.

"Don't you want to see your new house?"

"Yes," he said, but he didn't move.

Suzanne was trying to think of something to break through his shyness when she noticed the reptile prints on his shirt and glanced at his hat again. "There's a pond out back."

He lifted his gaze, intrigued. He looked so much like Rick it unnerved her.

"A pond?" he said. "Really?"

"Yes and you can see it clearly from one of the rooms upstairs. Would you like to see it?"

He nodded and took her hand with instant trust. Suzanne's heart shifted, surprised by the feel of his small hand in hers. She headed upstairs to one of the spare rooms.

"Where are you going?" Rick demanded when they were halfway up the stairs.

"To see the pond!" Luke said as though Suzanne was taking him to the circus. "Come, Daddy."

"Yes, Daddy," Suzanne teased, still trying to reconcile herself with his new role. "Come on."

Rick sent her a hooded look she couldn't interpret then followed them up the stairs.

"Where's Mandy?" Suzanne asked as she opened the door to one of the rooms.

"Somewhere," Rick said without much interest. "Don't worry, she'll find us."

"Yes, I suppose she's used to finding you in a bedroom."

Before Rick could reply, Luke ran to the window and stared at the pond enchanted. "I can see the pond. Daddy, look!"

Rick walked up to him and rested a hand on his shoulder. "I knew you would like it."

"You didn't tell me it had a pond."

"I wanted to surprise you."

Suzanne watched the pair with a slight ache of longing. They looked like the perfect picture of a father and his son and it was an intimate portrait where she didn't belong. She took a step back. "I'll leave you two and—"

Luke spun around with dismay. "No, don't go, Miss Suzanne."

Suzanne bit her lip finding no reason to stay, but Luke's liquid brown gaze softened her resolve. "Okay, I'll stay just a few minutes." She sat down on the bed, and before she could motion for him to sit besides her, he scrambled up on the bed and promptly sat on her lap. Suzanne looked at Rick for guidance, but he appeared as surprised by his son's boldness as she was.

"Luke, you're supposed to *ask* permission before you sit on someone's lap," he said.

"Miss Suzanne doesn't mind. She likes me." He looked up at her. "Right?"

"Right," she said, wondering if he were truly as shy as he'd first seemed.

"Can you tell me a story? Daddy says you know lots."

She glanced at Rick wondering what else he'd told his son. "I do."

"But you can only tell me your safe ones."

"My safe ones?"

"Yes." He giggled. "Granny says that you tell dirty stories, but I'm not big enough to hear them yet. And she says—"

Rick cleared his throat. "That's enough about Grandma. Let Miss Suzanne tell you a story."

"Okay."

Suzanne thought for a moment, then said, "Well, let me tell you how a pond came to be in our backyard. One day, when I was about your age, I wanted to go swimming, but I couldn't find any water. So I decided that I would make my own swimming pool. I found some of my mother's gardening tools in the barn and went out in search of the perfect place. When I found a small hole in the ground, already filled with some rainwater, I decided that that was where my swimming pool would be. I did some digging, a lot I thought at the time, and when I was finished I decided to try it out and go for a swim.

"Well, I'm sure I don't have to tell you that I got a lot of mud all over me. I had a great time, but when I tried to enter the kitchen, my mother screamed in horror at the sight of me covered in mud, and my dad had to take me out back and use a hose to wash me down. I cried and cried, because I couldn't understand why they were so angry. My dad kept asking me, 'What on earth were you doing, child?' In between my tears, I told him that I had gone swimming in my swimming pool.

"Well, later that day, my father found my swimming hole and hired a contractor to create a 'proper' pond for me to swim in. The contractor was the father of Billy Waxman, a boy in my class who liked me. When Billy found out that his father was making a pond for me, he had his dad fill it with goldfish and tadpoles. Billy was my first boyfriend. He liked me a lot and I liked him a lot. We were in first grade. So you see, you will be only the second little boy to play in the pond. Billy was the first."

"I want this to be *my* room," Luke said, scurrying off her lap.

"I'm glad you like it."

"I can wake up and see the pond every day."

"Yes, and there are frogs and snakes and fish."

"Really?"

"Yes. When I was a little girl I used to sit out there and play my violin." She lowered her voice to a whisper. "And sometimes, if you listened really carefully, you could hear the crickets play along with me."

Luke widened his eyes and said, "Can you play your violin for me so I can hear them?"

"It's been a long time and I'm sure the crickets are gone."

"You could make them come back. Maybe because they haven't heard the violin since you left so they went away. But when they hear it, maybe they will come again."

Suzanne sent Rick a rueful look. "Smart kid." She returned her gaze to Luke. "Maybe another time."

"When? Tomorrow?"

"No, but we'll see."

He pointed to an image on his shirt. "Do you know what this is?"

"No."

"It's a green tree frog." He pointed to another image. "And this is a spring pepper and this is a pig frog."

"Wow," Suzanne said, impressed.

Luke lifted his head, basking in her praise. "I can tell you the names of all the frogs on my shirt," he said. Smiling broadly, he pointed to each frog and told her its name.

"Good job," she said once he'd finished.

He leaned against her. "Daddy's gonna get me a book on crocodiles, but crocodiles don't live in ponds."

"No," Suzanne said in a soft voice. It was too comfortable being with him. His little body curled up against hers. He was not just any child, he was Rick's child. He smelled good and she could imagine tucking him into bed at night and kissing his forehead in the morning. "I'd better go," she said, desperate to escape. She stood and headed for the door despite Luke's cry of protest, but Mandy stopped her.

Chapter 10

"This is where you disappeared to," Mandy said, suddenly appearing in the doorway and blocking Suzanne's escape. "What ya'll looking at?"

"The pond," Suzanne said, reluctantly returning to the bed.

Mandy rolled her eyes. "That boy and his slimy creatures."

"This is going to be my room." Luke took Suzanne's hand. "Can you show me the pond, Miss Suzanne?"

She opened her mouth to reply, but Rick interrupted her.

"You can go with Mandy," he said. "I have to talk to Miss Suzanne first."

Luke began to scrunch up his face, ready to argue. "But I don't want to see the pond without Miss Suzanne."

Rick's voice remained firm. "Luke."

"We'll be right there," Suzanne quickly said, not wanting the boy to get into trouble, "and if you're good I'll show you the tadpoles."

He looked doubtful, as though he was used to disappointments. "You promise?"

"I do."

He folded his arms. "But I still—"

"One more word and I won't come down at all."

Luke sighed, acknowledging defeat. "All right," he said, leaving the room.

"Good job, Suzanne," Mandy said. "When he gets into his stubborn moods he's a nightmare. I doubt he'll sleep tonight after he sees this pond of yours." She followed him.

Suzanne smiled. "He may not want to leave."

"That's what I hope," Rick said.

Her smile dimmed. "Well, congratulations. He's wonderful."

"He's shy," Rick said, as though embarrassed to admit it.

"But he warms up quickly."

"Only to some." Rick shoved his hands in his pockets. "He's not usually this way. He likes you."

Suzanne dismissed his words with a wave of her hand. "He likes the fact that I have a pond."

"No, he likes *you*. I can tell the difference." He glanced out the window. "With most strangers he's mute and won't look up."

"Poor thing. He stood in the foyer as though he expected to get into trouble."

Rick sent her a sharp look. "I don't hit him."

Suzanne stared at Rick, surprised by his vehemence. "I didn't think you did."

He folded his arms and Suzanne could see where Luke had learned his defiant stance. "Why not? You know my past."

"Yes."

He studied her for a moment then let his arms fall to his sides. "And you never once thought—"

"That you'd hit a child or a woman? Never."

He looked at her unsure. "Even though I'm a Gordon?"

It was a loaded question that Suzanne refused to answer. She stood and gazed out the window, expertly changing the subject. "No one would think Luke was a Gordon with that shy personality. But I'm sure he'll grow out of it. He's smart and funny and definitely has your charm."

A proud grin touched Rick's mouth. "You liked him?"

She turned to him suddenly aware of how close he was to her, but she didn't move away. "Who wouldn't? If I had a son…" She bit her lip. "You and Mandy must be proud."

Rick looked out the window at Luke running to the pond. "I certainly am, but I don't know how Mandy feels. She's not his mother."

Suzanne didn't look at him. "She's not?"

"No."

"Where is his mother?"

He toyed with the cord for the blinds. "Don't know. Don't care."

"Doesn't he?"

"He doesn't remember her. She left when he was a year old. Look. The truth is I got careless and things happened. It was supposed to be a brief fling, but then she told me she was pregnant and I wasn't going to have my kid grow up without a father so I decided to marry her. After Luke was born I knew our marriage was a mistake so I paid her to disappear from our lives and she did."

Suzanne finally looked at him, shocked. "You paid her to disappear?"

"She would have eventually, it just would have taken longer."

"I can't believe she'd abandon her child."

Rick stared down at her with amusement. "If you knew her you'd believe it. I met her at a high society gathering. She pressed a pair of black lace panties into my hand and I took her up on her offer. I was flattered that a woman like her would take interest in me. I was reckless back then." He rested his shoulder against the wall. "But that's no surprise to you. You never expected much of men. Especially me. No one did."

"I never said that."

"Some things don't need to be said."

"Well you're wrong, but I'm not going to try to convince you."

He shrugged. "I can't say I'm proud of what happened. I was stupid."

"Meaning?"

"Meaning, what was supposed to be a one-night stand dragged on for nearly two years because I wasn't paying attention. But I don't regret getting Luke out of it."

"Good."

He searched her gaze and soon the very air around them seemed electrified. She lowered her eyes. "So now you have Mandy who is more of the motherly type."

He nodded. "Yes, I pay her to be."

She looked up at him again and frowned. "Pay her? What is it with you and money?"

"She's Luke's nanny." He smiled at her expression. "Who did you think she was?"

"You know who I thought she was." Suzanne paused. "But she's not very good."

"What do you mean?"

"If she's his nanny, she shouldn't have forgotten him in the foyer."

"She didn't forget him. She just doesn't want to hover over him. He tends to freeze in new situations, but eventually recovers."

Suzanne didn't agree, but shrugged. "Doesn't matter anyway. I'm sure you'll be happy here."

Rick's gaze grew serious. "Actually it does matter. I brought Luke here for a reason. I wanted you to meet him."

"Why? You needed something else to brag about?"

"I think we can help each other."

Suzanne shook her head. "The answer is no."

"You don't even know what I'm going to say."

"No, but I already think it's a bad idea. It has to be. It's yours, after all."

"At least let me finish."

She shrugged and folded her arms. "Fine. Go ahead."

"I've got money and I can clear all your debts and you'll be free to write. In exchange I ask for only one favor."

She looked at him, wary. "Can I say no now?"

"Suzanne," he said with warning.

"What's the favor?"

"Marry me."

Her arms fell to her side. She'd imagined him saying many things, but not that. "What?"

"I'm asking you to marry me."

"Are you crazy?"

He held up his hand. "Hear me out. I don't care how people treat me in this town, but I do care how they treat Luke. With you as his stepmother he'll meet the right people and grow up the way he should. I want to give Luke all the benefits I didn't have."

"But there are plenty of other women—"

"They are not who I want. I want someone who knows the ins and outs of this town, how this house should be run. I want someone who has your reputation and history."

"Della would marry you in a second." She snapped her fingers.

"I want someone with half a brain." He shook his head. "You're perfect. You have the right name."

She laughed. "That name may not mean as much anymore. Especially because of the book."

"It's still better than mine. You know this can work. You've got the style and class that I don't have and in this town that matters more than money. People respect you." He rubbed the back of his neck. "And I'd take care of you."

"I can take care of myself."

"I need your help."

She headed for the door. "No, you don't."

"Don't think of me, think of Luke. Help me take care of him."

She halted in the doorway. He was offering her a

chance she'd stopped allowing herself to dream about. To be a mother. But at what price? "I promised I'd never marry again."

"This would be different."

Suzanne slowly turned to him. "How?" she said bitterly. "I didn't marry Wallace for love, either."

He closed the distance between them. "I'll never cheat on you. I'll never shame you." He touched her face. "And it may be a loveless marriage, but it won't be a passionless one." He lowered his voice. "Trust me. Don't think. Just say yes."

"Rick! Suzanne!" Mandy called from the bottom of the stairs. "Aren't you coming?"

"What's your answer?" Rick's dark eyes pierced hers with a magnetic intensity that held her captive.

"I don't know."

"Yes, you do."

"Mandy's waiting."

"Let her wait."

She turned to the door and shouted, "We'll be there." Then she looked at Rick and said, "Please give me time," before running down the stairs, desperate to break his invisible hold.

Suzanne had to hide her shock when she saw the condition of the pond. She hadn't looked at it since her return. It was overgrown with weeds and the top of the water was covered with a thin film of plankton or some other form of water life. Initially she couldn't see anything living, then Luke screamed out with excitement.

"Look! Look! I see a tadpole!" His enthusiasm only grew after that. They spent another hour at the pond where he pointed out all the living creatures he could find. There were the three large bullfrogs sitting on a giant stone in the middle of the pond, a harmless garden snake that slithered over his shoes, a pod of tadpoles, several large goldfish, which had somehow survived the neglect, and dragonflies jumping on the water lilies, which her mother had planted, to make the unsightly pond, as she referred to it, more "presentable."

"It's time to go," Rick said.

Luke turned to his father, upset. "Already?"

"Yes."

Suzanne tickled him under his chin before he could argue. "Don't worry, the pond is all yours now." She stood and walked toward the house. "Come on."

He ran up to her and grabbed her hand. "I still don't want to leave yet."

"You'll be back soon."

"Can I spend the night with you?"

Rick stared at his son, stunned, but Suzanne laughed. "You are your father's child and may be not as shy as we think. I'm sorry, perhaps another time."

"That means no," he said disappointedly, then followed Mandy to the car.

"How about an answer to my question," Rick said as Suzanne climbed the porch steps.

She looked at him as she gripped the railing. "I told you I need time."

He took two steps until they were at eye level. "I gave you over an hour. What's your reply? What do I get to tell Luke?"

Suzanne frowned. "You play dirty."

He let his finger trail a sensuous path down her arm. "At one time you liked how I played."

"That time is gone."

His finger trailed up. "So you're turning me down?"

She folded her arms, her skin tingling. "No."

He stilled. "You're saying yes?"

"On one condition."

"I plan to sleep with you."

Her cheeks burned. "That wasn't the condition."

"I just wanted to make sure we understand each other." He took another step toward her. "What's the condition?"

"That you won't shame me. If I hear even a whisper that you're seeing another woman it's over between us."

"I told you—"

"I know what you told me, but I want you to promise."

He wrapped an arm around her waist. "So you do believe in men's promises."

"Just say it."

He slid another arm around her. "Okay. I promise that you'll be the only woman in my life." He placed a kiss on her cheek. "And I promise that you'll have no reason to doubt me." He kissed her other cheek. "And one day I promise to make you believe every word I've said." He bent to kiss her lips, but she pulled away.

"Mandy and Luke could see us."

"So what? I'm not going to be your little secret again. If you plan to marry me, accept me as I am."

"I do."

"Then kiss me now."

She planned to kiss him quickly, but the moment her lips touched his he didn't allow her to escape and deepened the kiss with a mastery that made her head spin. When he finally withdrew she was breathless.

"I'll call you tomorrow," he said, and leaped over the railing, landing smoothly on the ground. He turned to her and his face broke into a smile. "You won't regret this."

"Are you sure this is what you want?"

He responded with a wink that said it all, turned and dashed to his car.

Suzanne waved as they drove off, knowing that she wasn't saying goodbye but "see you soon." In an instant she'd changed her life. She'd closed the door to leaving this town, to protecting her heart against Rick. She knew from the first moment she saw him that she loved Luke and the thought of being his mother was a thrill. That didn't scare her. Loving a child was easy. What did scare her was that she was in danger of falling in love with his father, too.

Chapter 11

Frieda inhaled her fourth cigarette while staring blankly out the window, waiting for Rick's visit. She glanced at her watch with impatience then took a swig of whiskey. Good company was few and far between nowadays and she'd never admit to it, but she looked forward to her son's visits. Sometimes he brought his son—or what he tried to pass off as one, she thought with a sniff as she twirled the liquid in her glass. The boy was too soft and quiet for her taste. Not like the brash, loud man her husband had been. Not that she missed the bastard, just the company.

When the phone rang she stubbed out her cigarette on the arm of her recliner's plastic cover and answered.

"Is it settled?" a familiar voice asked.

"Yes, the house is ours. He signed the papers."

"So it's a done deal," Wallace said.

"That's right."

"And you plan to hold up your end of the bargain?"

"Don't I always? Why do you want her back?"

"That's my business. I just want to make sure the way is clear for me."

"Yes. Without the house I'm sure she'll fall right back into your arms." Frieda paused when she heard a car. "Rick's back. Gotta go."

"He still doesn't know anything?"

"No."

"Good." Wallace disconnected.

Frieda hung up the phone and quickly put the whiskey away. Rick hated seeing her drink. She smoothed down her dress, picked up a magazine and sat back in the recliner, so that when Rick entered the room she looked the picture of domestic tranquility. "You're late," she said. "I've been waiting."

He kissed her on the cheek. "Hello, Momma."

"Do you know what time it is?"

"I told you we went to visit Suzanne."

"Where's Luke?"

"At the hotel."

"Why didn't you bring him by?"

"You'll see him next time."

She tossed the magazine on the ground. "So you let Suzanne meet that little girl you're raising?"

Rick wiped crumbs from off the couch cushion and sat. "Luke is just shy."

"As shy as a virgin in a biker bar. He needs some balls."

Rick picked up the magazine and set it on the side table. "He's only five."

"Nearly six. You were further along at that age."

"He's not me."

"You're sure he's yours?"

"He's mine and we're not having this conversation again."

Frieda shrugged and grabbed a chip from the bag on the cluttered coffee table.

Rick frowned at the mess. "I thought I arranged a housekeeper to come every week."

"I can keep my own house. Besides, they steal."

Rick didn't reply. Of all people, his mother would know about the habits of some housekeepers. She'd been one for ten years. Unfortunately, his older brother had gotten his sticky fingers from her and had landed in prison twice.

"When is she moving out?" Frieda asked.

"She's not."

Her heart began to race. "What do you mean? The house deal didn't go through or something?"

"It went through. The house is mine."

She looked at him with confusion. "I don't understand. Is she going to rent a room?"

"She's going to be my wife."

Frieda snatched another cigarette from her carton and lit it. "You always did have a nasty sense of humor."

"I'm not kidding."

She stared at him, stunned. "You're serious."

"Yes, I'm going to marry her."

"How do you know she'll marry you? Just because you got money doesn't mean she'll lower her standards."

"She already has."

Frieda gripped her cigarette, unaware of the ashes falling to the floor. "She said yes?"

Rick nodded.

Frieda took a long drag of her cigarette, her hand shaking as she thought of the phone call she'd just received. "She must be more desperate than I thought." She exhaled, trying to think of what she would say to Wallace. "Did she convince you of this?"

"No, it was my idea."

"Why the hell do you want to marry her? Remember how she treated you?"

Rick ignored the second question. "She'll be good for Luke."

"I know you need help with that—" she stopped when she saw Rick's face and knew this was no time for teasing "—with Luke, but you don't need a Rand. She's got you in her claws again and you're too stupid to see it."

"I'm doing exactly what I planned to do."

"You didn't tell me."

He tugged on the strap of his watch. "No, but you'll get used to the idea."

"You're making a mistake. Think this through. There are other people who—" She halted and concentrated on her cigarette, letting the smoke burn her lungs and the nicotine ease her worry.

"What other people?" Rick demanded.

She waved her hand in a dismissive manner. "Nothing."

"This is my business and no one else's."

"Why don't you marry that ninny you hired?"

"She's a nanny and she's family."

"A distant cousin, thank God, and I meant what I said

the first time. She's as empty-headed as they come but I guess you're satisfied with the way she looks after the boy."

"She's temporary."

"Then make her permanent," Frieda demanded.

"Calm down. Do you want to have another stroke?"

"It wasn't a stroke," she grumbled. "It was a TIA, a ministroke."

"I don't care what it was. I don't want to go through that again." He shook his head. "I didn't expect you to be happy, but you're taking this a little too hard. What's going on?"

"Don't do this, Rickie."

"Why not?"

"I told you why not."

"Not every reason."

She picked up her ashtray and tapped her cigarette against it. "Suzanne's a traitor. That book—"

"I don't care about the book."

She pointed her cigarette at him. "You should care. What if she starts writing about—"

"It doesn't matter. In a few days you're going to have a new daughter-in-law so start getting used to it. It's done, Momma."

"She might not show up."

"I'll make sure she does." He stood. "I'd better go." He bent to kiss her on the forehead but she turned away.

"Just go," she said and kept her face turned until she heard the front door close. The moment he was gone, Frieda began to pace. This wasn't what she'd planned. This would ruin everything. How could Rick marry Suzanne? A *Rand?* She hated the Rands and everything they represented. They were liars and destroyers. Her life would have been different if it hadn't been for them. She could have made something of herself if their influence and power in the town hadn't been so fierce. Gerald Rand had sent her son to prison, instead of giving him leniency. Malcolm was a good boy deep down, but the Rands didn't care and putting him away had taken from them the extra income they needed and had forced Rick to work two jobs.

And that harlot of a daughter had used him. She remembered her coming by wanting to speak to him, but she wasn't going to let Suzanne anywhere near her son if she could help it. And she did. Frieda was glad when Suzanne married and Rick moved away. But then she wrote that book and Suzanne made her hate the Rands all over again. How dare she profit off of their pain, and now she'd captured Rick's heart again. Suzanne was supposed to be free for Wallace. She had to think. She pulled out her whiskey bottle and poured herself a drink. She finished it in one long swallow and picked up the phone. When the line connected she said, "There may be a problem."

Wallace hung up the phone after talking to Frieda, then burst into laughter. The old woman had to be mistaken. Suzanne would never marry Gordon. And he'd done his best to make sure. She'd accepted his gifts and seemed intrigued when he'd talked about Gordon's intentions regarding 468 Trellis Court. He would have had her already, if her friends hadn't stopped by. And he would have her no matter what. He didn't just want her back. He needed her back.

It wasn't until after their divorce that he learned how

much the success of his practice depended on her. How much he'd listened to her quiet advice. How much he'd depended on her clever mind and keen observation to handle a client or a case. He never paid her a salary, because she was his wife, and he didn't feel he had to since he provided for her.

Gerald Rand had taught his daughter well, and he'd handed him a cash cow that he'd let slip through his fingers. He should have followed Rand's advice and been more discreet, but he'd been arrogant and as the years passed Suzanne made sure his bed became colder than an icebox. He'd thought of divorcing her during that difficult time, but his old man hadn't wanted him to. He liked Suzanne and liked his association with Gerald Rand even more.

Wallace knew this and lived his life to make his old man proud so he kept the marriage up. More times than not Wallace had felt like a pale imitation to his brilliant father until he'd developed his ability to listen and uncover people's weak spots. Soon that trait served him well and impressed his father and improved his business, but it hadn't saved his marriage.

Wallace let his good humor subside and rubbed his chin, pensive. He should have worked harder at keeping Suzanne. He hadn't expected paying alimony to be such a pain. At first it hadn't bothered him. Then she wrote a book and became a celebrity. He'd helped her get there, with his information about certain people in town, but she kept all the glory for herself. But now, he had even more information—the type that affected Suzanne personally and Frieda had given it to him when she'd appeared in his office over a month ago asking for a favor.

"You know Suzanne is coming back to town?" she said, sitting in her chair as though ready to spring out of it.

Wallace stared at the older woman with boredom. His father had told him that in the past she'd been a good lay, but he couldn't imagine that now. However, he'd been taught to respect his elders so he continued to listen. "Everybody knows that. She has to take care of her father's estate."

"Rick wants to buy the house from her."

"So?"

"That's the only exchange I want between them. I'm wondering if you could make sure of that."

He sat up, interested. "You think there's something going on between them?"

"No, but Suzanne is dangerous. She tricked my son once and I won't see that happen again. I could make this worth your while."

The prospect of money always caught Wallace's attention and he needed money to take care of some heavy debts. "I'm listening…"

And he listened for over an hour as Frieda told him all he needed to know to keep Gordon in line. Too bad she didn't know how much that would cost her.

Claudia and Noreen stared at Suzanne as though she'd just announced she was flying to the moon. They sat in a fashionable restaurant in Raleigh, while the remnants of their meal lay abandoned on the table.

"You're getting married?" Claudia said just to make sure she'd heard correctly.

Suzanne nodded. "Yes."

Noreen adjusted her glasses. "To Rick Gordon."

"Yes," she repeated.

"The man who bought your house?" Claudia said.

"Yes."

"The same one who broke your heart?" Noreen added.

"I know it sounds a little strange," Suzanne admitted.

"It sounds absolutely crazy."

"Don't we get a chance to meet him first?" Claudia asked.

"There's not enough time," Suzanne said.

"Make time."

"I don't want to," she snapped.

Noreen stared at her, surprised by her forcefulness, but Claudia smiled. "Wow, Suzanne's getting some fire."

Suzanne stared at Noreen helplessly. "Don't be angry."

"I'm not angry, I'm worried."

Claudia toyed with her straw, bobbing it up and down in her glass. "I can't believe you're marrying the man you wrote about in your book."

"I only based the character on him," Suzanne corrected, wishing she hadn't shared the basis for her inspiration.

"You named him Roland Grant."

"So what?"

Claudia ignored her. "Noreen, you should be taking notes. This would be a great plot for one of your books."

Noreen frowned. "It's irrational. Personally, I think it's more in your arena. Isn't there some psychosis for an author who falls in love with her creation?"

"I'm not in love with him," Suzanne said, waving her arms to dismiss the idea. "And the man in the book is *not* Rick. It's just a representation."

"It's close enough. He's a heartbreaker."

"I plan to keep my heart safe. I know what I'm doing."

Noreen closed her eyes, as though in pain. "You haven't thought this through." She looked at her, puzzled. "Do you want another divorce?"

Suzanne rested her arms on the table and said in a low voice. "He has a son."

"So?"

Claudia began to smile with understanding. "Oh, I see."

Noreen shook her head. "I don't."

"She wants a child."

Noreen widened her eyes, outraged by Claudia's reasoning. "There are other ways to have children without a man involved." She touched Suzanne's hand. "I could give you a list. The options are amazing."

Suzanne pulled her hand away with a laugh. "It's okay, Noreen I haven't lost my mind. I want to do this."

"You may want the child, but do you realize you're *marrying* his father? Marriage is marriage no matter what the reason."

Suzanne picked up a grilled zucchini stick and dipped it in the cheese sauce. "We tried to get married once before."

"What?" Noreen said.

Claudia added more sugar to her iced tea. "How?"

Suzanne picked up her napkin and wiped her fingers. "We tried to get pregnant. We were young and it seemed like a good idea at the time. If I got pregnant then Rick would have to marry me and no one could stop us from being together and we'd be free. But that never happened."

"It still may not have worked out," Noreen said. "But Suzanne, marriage is different than dating."

"I know. I've done it before."

Claudia sat back. "It's not a shotgun wedding, but you're still getting the man you wanted."

Noreen wiped her glasses with the hem of her shirt. "I just hope nothing goes wrong."

"Nothing will go wrong," Suzanne said, hoping she was right.

For the next several weeks, Suzanne's schedule focused on fixing up the house for her new family. With Rick's unlimited bank account, she was able to hire one of the most premiere interior design firms in the area. Everything was redone to reflect their new lives. One particular project took precedent—Luke's bedroom. Because she knew about his love for amphibians and other water creatures, she worked with designers to create a themed room.

After doing some research and contacting the Durham National Zoo, the designers created a special artificial lagoon in Luke's bedroom. And when Luke finally saw it his face lit up.

"Wow. This is cool!" he had said and then dashed over to his greatest surprise—a large amphibian tank. Luke could not contain himself as he pressed his face against the glass of the enclosure, which was separated in two. On one side he could see several gray tree frogs, a small box turtle; on the other side a garter snake and two red-backed salamanders.

"That's a tree frog!" he said, barely able to contain himself.

Suzanne nodded. "Yes."

"Why is it not moving?"

"It is just relaxing and enjoying itself."

He pointed. "What is that one?"

"Don't tap the glass, honey. It's called a box turtle."

He snatched his hand back. "Will it bite me?"

"No. I'll show you how to pick it up and take care of it." As he moved slowly around the tank, Luke suddenly let out a high shriek. "Look at the snake! Look at the snake! Wow! That's cool. Can it kill you?"

"Oh, no. It is not poisonous."

"What is poisonous?"

"That means it has something inside it that could kill you. It won't hurt you."

As he looked closer, he saw something moving under a batch of fake leaves. "What is that flat thing?"

"It's a salamander."

"A sal-man-da?"

"No, a sal-la-man-der."

"Oh, a sal-man-ner!"

"Yes."

Rick came up behind them and shook his head. "Amazing."

The aquarium was artfully decorated to provide round-the-year shelter for its inhabitants. In the winter, the snakes and box turtle could find small holes and large rocks to hibernate. The spotted salamander and the "masked" wood frog could find small pieces of fake rotting logs and layers of old leaves to hibernate. Since it was summer, a labyrinth of twigs, small plants and fake rocks provided ample place for them to sun themselves under the direct sun rays that came through the large bedroom window and the artificial sunlamps.

"You didn't have to do all this," Rick said, looking at the mural on the wall that replicated an underwater cave, then the library of books on water creatures, and a lighted globe.

Suzanne shrugged, although she was pleased with his praise. "It's your money."

"But you're the one who made my son happy."

Luke hugged her leg. "I have the best room in the whole wide world. Thank you, Momma."

"You're welcome," Suzanne said in an unsteady voice.

Luke ran over to his bed, grabbed a stuffed snake and started to make hissing noises.

Rick looked at her, curious. "You don't mind, do you? I can have him call you something else."

"No, it's fine. I was just surprised. We're not married yet."

"Yes, and I plan to change that very soon."

Although she knew the day would come, her heart still jumped to her throat. There was no turning back now. In two days she would be married.

Chapter 12

"I won't marry you."

Suzanne stared at the judge, dumbfounded. She and Rick stood in the courthouse before the Honorable Judge Jean Meadows while Luke and Mandy sat on the bench behind them. The judge was a formidable woman with a voice that belonged on radio. Her words were an unexpected development for such an extraordinary day, which started with Rick arriving on Suzanne's doorstep.

"So you showed up," she said when she saw him.

His gaze swept her cream-colored dress with admiration. "Nothing could keep me away."

"You don't have to worry. I'm very good at getting married."

"I know. I was at your wedding."

She blinked. "No, you weren't."

"Not as a guest, but as one of the help, which is no big surprise."

"I didn't know."

"I didn't want you to know. And just as I predicted you made a beautiful bride."

"And now?"

His gaze measured her form. "Nothing's changed."

"Yes, well as we both know, getting married is easy. It's staying married that's hard."

"It won't be hard for us."

"You sound certain."

"I am. There's no one to get in our way this time."

But apparently he was wrong. Suzanne looked at her old family friend and knew that somehow luck was not on their side. "Excuse me?" she said, unsure she'd heard correctly.

"You might as well go home because I won't marry you. You may have lost your mind, but I certainly haven't. Your father would turn over in his grave if he knew you planned to shackle yourself to this man." She gestured to Rick. "Yes, he may be handsome and now he's got some money in his pockets, but I knew his father and the apple doesn't fall far from the tree."

"I'm nothing like my father," Rick said.

"How about your brother, then?" she countered.

Rick opened his mouth to reply, but Suzanne took his hand and stopped him.

Jean looked at Suzanne's gesture with disgust. "Yes, you'll have to keep him in line. He doesn't drink, but I remember him as a boy and a young man and I know what he's trying to set up. He's marrying you for your reputation and to help him raise his little bastard."

Rick narrowed his eyes and said with a cold note of warning, "Watch your words, Judge."

She ignored him as though he were a cockroach who'd scurried into her courtroom. "You think you had trouble with Wallace? Do you honestly expect this one to be loyal to you?"

"Yes," Suzanne said as Rick stood stiff beside her.

"And he won't touch you?"

Feeling Rick's anger, Suzanne squeezed his hand and calmly said, "No."

"Liquor can change a man."

"I don't drink," Rick said.

"I trust him," Suzanne added.

"So you say," Jean said with an ugly smile. "but that doesn't matter. You may want to ruin your life, but I'm not going to help you."

"It's your obligation."

The judge smiled. "Want to sue me?"

Rick began to turn. "Let's go somewhere else."

Suzanne didn't move. "We're staying right here." She looked at Jean and remembered the judge's many visits to her house. She'd been an attorney then. There had been rumors that she'd been one of her father's mistresses, but Suzanne had never believed it. Now she wasn't so sure. However, as she looked at Jean she didn't see an adversary. She saw a woman who cared. Jean had also been at Melba's trial and Suzanne remembered the tears she refused to let fall as Melba's sentence was read. But Suzanne wasn't Melba or the woman she'd been before. She had to let Jean know she could take care of herself. "Have you forgotten who I am?"

Jean's smile fell. "Of course, I know—"

"Actually, I don't believe you know as much as you need to or you wouldn't be wasting our time. My name is Suzanne Rand and my father was a judge and my ex-husband was an attorney. I may not have gotten a degree but living with those two men in the legal field taught me a few things about the law and my rights. This is Rick Gordon the owner of a multimillion-dollar business with access to a team of top-notch lawyers. Now we want to get married today and you will comply or regret that you even woke up this morning. Am I clear?"

"Now, Suzanne—"

"I asked you a question."

"Yes, you're clear," the judge said grimly. She tapped her desk with reluctant admiration. "I read that book of yours and real life doesn't tie up as sweet and pretty as a story."

"I know."

The judge looked at Rick then Suzanne with a shrewd gaze. "They said you came back different."

"They were right. Now let's proceed."

"Hmm, maybe I'm warning the wrong half of this pair." Jean adjusted her glasses and turned her attention to Rick, finally addressing him as an equal. "You sure you want to go through with this?"

Rick sent her a glare so cold she nearly choked. She cleared her throat. "Very well," she said then started the proceedings.

Suzanne left the courtroom still unable to grasp the choice she'd made. It was eerie being in the courthouse again. It was like stepping into her past. This courthouse had been her second home. So many lives had been changed there—one being Melba Lowell's. She and Rick had been in the courthouse together, but were separated by class, family and duty. In a strange way the Lowells had brought them together and torn them apart. She remembered seeing Rick with his mother and those who were on Melba's side during her trial for killing her husband. Suzanne had wanted to talk to him then. They were only a few yards away from each other, but it felt like miles. Who would have thought that years later they'd enter the same courthouse and leave it as husband and wife? What would her parents say? What would the town say?

She turned to Rick and he looked like someone hiding secret thoughts.

The wedding ceremony was so different from her first. Her first had been a huge ordeal with more than three hundred guests, an orchestra and dozens and dozens of flowers everywhere. But the one similarity between the past and present was that the man beside her didn't love her. At least she wasn't naive this time. Suzanne didn't expect anything. She thought about Jean's words—was she being foolish again? Dare she trust him? Did he even care? Just like Wallace, all he wanted from her was her name. Her gaze fell to Luke, and his wide smile gave her strength. His warmth and acceptance made all the difference. Motherhood was something she'd wanted and now she had that chance. Luke would be the one man who would eventually love and trust her.

"Let's go get ice cream," she said, referring to the ice

cream parlor off the main street in town. For weeks she'd rarely ventured into town, especially in the daytime, but now she knew she was ready.

Rick came out of his thoughts and looked at Mandy. "Yes, go ahead, we'll join you."

Suzanne looked at him with concern. "What's wrong?"

"I didn't get you a present."

She blinked at his strange reply. "I don't need one. Besides I didn't get you anything, either."

He rubbed the back of his neck with agitation. "Why didn't you turn away?"

"What?"

"That judge gave you every reason not to marry me and you still did. Why?"

"You can't let Jean bother you."

He repeated his question. "Why, Suzanne?"

"Rick, it's no big deal."

He stopped walking. "Answer my question."

"Why does it matter?"

"It does. Why did you still marry me?"

She threw up her hands, exasperated. "Because of Luke."

He searched her face, his tone intense. "That's all?"

"Did you expect another reason?"

He sighed and his gaze fell. "No." He turned. "Of course not."

"Because the other reason is that I wanted to."

He spun around. "You mean that?"

"Yes."

"You don't have to love me, but I'm glad that you want me."

"What woman doesn't want you?"

"I only care about one." His mouth covered hers with such force that she stumbled back and had to hold on to him to keep from falling.

"Rick," she breathed when he briefly drew away for air. "We can't kiss like this here."

"I'm kissing my bride. What's wrong with that?"

She couldn't come up with a response and soon she didn't care. Normally, she didn't believe in public displays of affection, but somehow she knew this was special—important. This was their first kiss as husband and wife. She let herself relax into his arms.

"Hey, what's this?" Wallace said, appearing suddenly from one of the rooms. "Moving in on my territory, Gordon?"

"The only territory here belongs to me."

Suzanne held up her hands. "I'm no one's territory."

The two men ignored her.

"You're trying to stake claim?" Wallace said.

"I've already got the deed. She's my wife."

Wallace stared at Suzanne. "You're kidding me. You really went through with it?"

"You knew?"

"I heard rumors. You can't start redecorating your house without some talk slipping out."

"Where did you hear the rumors?" Suzanne asked.

"People," he said vaguely. "But I didn't believe it. I thought you had better taste."

"Go away, Wallace."

He ignored her and addressed Rick. "Heard you had a kid and we all know you need someone for him, but don't expect any more. She's as barren as a dried up well. Isn't that right, Suzanne?"

Suzanne gritted her teeth, but Rick grinned. "Are you sure you weren't shooting blanks, Lyon?"

Wallace's face went deep red. "Don't mess with me, Gordon. I know things that could break up this little union."

"Like what?"

"Ask your momma."

Suzanne gripped Rick's arm. "Let's go. He's just trying to goad you."

Rick sent Wallace a look, then allowed Suzanne to drag him away.

"Forget about him. Don't let him ruin this day."

But Suzanne knew he'd already ruined it. She was well acquainted with Wallace's underhanded ways. His father had been the prosecutor at Melba's trial and he'd done a successful smear campaign. The Lyons could be dirty when they wanted something and his father had wanted Melba proven guilty and he'd won. She remembered the cries of outrage and the shouts of triumph when the verdict came down. She remembered seeing Melba being led away. Her former music teacher showed no reaction to the verdict and looked like the cold, heartless murderer they'd portrayed her to be. But Suzanne knew that wasn't true. Later Melba would die in prison from ovarian cancer after completing four years of her thirty years to life sentence. But in a way she'd died the day she was convicted, maybe even before that.

Suzanne was eager to leave the courthouse and welcome the sight of the sun outside. She opened the door and seconds later a camera flashed. "Tell us about this special day," a reporter said.

"I see news still travels fast in Anadale," Suzanne said.

"Hey, every small town needs its celebrities and this story is hot. We already have three headlines," said the wiry man with a large camera slung around his neck.

"I won't even ask how you found out." She glanced at Wallace as he got into his car.

"Can't share my source."

"We'll give you the details another time," Rick said.

"I hope so. My editor wants something on the front page and if it's not your story it will be *a* story."

"One filled with rumors and gossip?" Suzanne guessed, knowing how the local paper operated.

"One that will sell papers." The reporter handed Suzanne his card. "You have twenty-four hours," he said before leaving.

Rick took the card and shoved it in his pocket. "He'll wait."

Suzanne opened her mouth to reply then saw Luke sitting on the front courthouse steps while Mandy spoke to a guard. Suzanne went up to her, politely told the guard they had to go, and said to Mandy, "What happened to the ice cream?"

"Oh, I was going to get it, but that nice young man started to tell me about when this courthouse was built and I just love history and—"

"Fine, you can go and continue that conversation. We're leaving." She held her hand out to Luke. "Come on, we're going into town." She walked away and didn't notice Rick saying something to Mandy before he joined her.

"You're going to have to let her go," she said. "I wouldn't trust her to watch a school of fish."

"I know, but she's family and needed the work and you have to help family."

Suzanne sent him a curious look. "How many family members are you helping?"

"Enough," Rick said, not wanting to elaborate, but Suzanne could hear the burden in his voice. He was the "successful one" and his obligation was clear. "She's the last one and I got her on short notice."

"Why did you need her on short notice?"

"I had to fire the last nanny on the spot."

"Why?" Suzanne asked, intrigued by his vagueness.

He glanced at his son then lowered his voice. "She was starting to get ideas that our relationship could be something more."

"Oh."

"It's happened a few times."

Suzanne flashed a sly grin. "I thought you'd have fun with that."

"Not when I have a business to run."

"Why not hire a man, then?"

He glanced away. "I did once."

The way he said the words made her look closely at him and she saw a tinge of red in his cheeks. "He fell for you?"

Rick studied a passing car.

Suzanne burst into laughter.

"It's not funny."

She laughed harder and Rick couldn't help a smile. "It was very awkward."

Suzanne covered her mouth, trying to contain herself. "I can imagine." At that thought she burst into fresh peals of laughter. Eventually she sobered. "I guess I'm helping you in more ways than one."

"Yes."

Suzanne spotted a drugstore. "I need to stop in there for a few things before we get the ice cream. Okay?"

Suzanne entered the store and grabbed a basket. She hadn't gone in since her return and not much had changed. It still had a country charm. She saw the clerk, Hannah Fulford, and in a flash the image of a young girl in a short pink dress entered her mind, but quickly vanished. Unlike her cousin, she didn't look as though she'd ever entered a salon, keeping her hair and features natural. But the years had been kind to her and, though she no longer wore short dresses, her khaki trousers and linen blouse emphasized an attractive figure. However, Suzanne could see that her feelings for Rick had not changed because she cast a wary eye on Rick and Luke, but when she saw Suzanne she smiled. "Suzanne! Nice to see you here. You haven't been in town much."

"No, I've been busy."

Luke picked up a candy bar.

Hannah scowled. "Put that back, you little thief."

Startled by her harsh words, Luke quickly placed the candy back on the shelf. "I wasn't going to steal it," he cried.

"Why are you harassing my son?" Rick asked.

"He was going to put that candy bar in his pocket. I saw him."

"You didn't see anything."

"Everyone knows that Gordons are nothing more than thieves and drunkards."

Suzanne set a box of tissues into her basket. "You're calling my son a thief?"

Hannah blanched. "Your son?"

"Yes," she said without explanation. Obviously the gossip about them hadn't reached everyone in town yet.

Hannah looked at Luke, clearly perplexed. "He belongs to you?"

"Yes."

She pointed to Rick. "But I thought—"

"Yes, I know what you thought. Is my family welcome here or not?"

"Well of course any Rand—"

"You mean Gordon."

"What?"

"My name is now Suzanne Gordon."

"Since when?" Hannah demanded.

"Today."

"You've got to be kidding me," she said with both surprise and disgust. "I go on a two-week vacation and something like this happens?" She came around the counter and dragged Suzanne into a corner. "You're making the same mistake. I warned you about Wallace years ago and I'm warning you now. Rick's no good. I know of his charm and fell for it years ago."

"It's different now."

"He goes through women like his father went through whiskey. Annul this marriage or else."

"Or else what?"

Hannah tilted her head to the side. "I thought you were a smart woman, but if I have to spell things out for you I will. Your book was bad enough, but this is going to ruin your reputation. You're going to be the town's pariah. You haven't raised his status, you've lowered yours."

Suzanne set her basket down, ready to leave. "I guess I'll take my business elsewhere. Come, Luke—" She took the boy's hand and left.

"I thought you were going to buy something," Rick said.

"I changed my mind."

Rick shoved his hands in his pockets. "What did she say to you?"

"Nothing."

"Don't start this marriage by lying to me."

"She basically said what Jean said."

He pulled on his chin. "She tried to warn you off me."

"Yes."

"Don't let her get to you."

Suzanne tried, but couldn't help it as they walked down the main street. Some things about the town had changed but so much hadn't, like the people.

"Why did you come back here?" she asked.

"Why did you?"

"You know why. I had no choice, but you did—do. How can you take the way people treat you? First Jean implying that you would hit me, knowing how I felt about Mr. Lowell and Melba—"

"It's okay."

She glanced down at the little boy beside her and lowered her voice. "And to call him a bastard?"

"Suzanne—"

"Then Hannah calls him a thief? I don't understand how you can take the snide comments and cold stares. It was bad enough for me, but I didn't know you…" She shook her head with frustration. "Do you think it's wise to expose him to this?"

"That's why I have you. You'll help me change that. You already have."

She stopped in front of the ice cream parlor. "No, I haven't," she said, going inside. She let Luke order a bubblegum sundae, and then they sat outside with their cones. They ate in silence. Mandy joined them and offered to take Luke to the park. Suzanne began to protest, but Rick agreed and the two left.

"Why do you think nothing's changed?" he asked Suzanne. He held up his hands. "Forget it, I don't want to know. Don't worry about Hannah. She's just angry with me and we both know you have more connections than she does."

He was right, but it didn't feel like enough and she couldn't help wondering what happened between them. "There are plenty of other places to raise your son. Places that aren't as small-minded as here."

"It's home to me and there are decent people here. Don't confuse the town with what happened to Melba. Twelve people sent her away, but there were plenty of others who were on her side."

"If you care about the town so much, why did you leave?"

He sent her a sharp look. "There was no reason to stay."

"And you have one now?"

"Yes, don't you?"

She nodded, but without conviction. "I suppose."

"I guess the Gordon stain is already getting to you. Do you want to go back to meeting in dark places and hiding in my old man's car?"

"Be serious."

He rested an arm on her shoulders. "I never said being married to me would be easy."

"What happened between you and Hannah?" she couldn't help asking.

"She did a foolish thing."

"What?"

"She fell in love with me."

"Oh," Suzanne said, knowing she was in danger of being just as foolish.

Chapter 13

"I saw them at the courthouse," Wallace told Frieda over the phone the moment he got in his car. "The marriage is a done deal."

"Don't worry, it won't last."

"You sound certain."

"I am."

He adjusted his visor to block out the sun. "I don't care as long as I get my money."

"Why should I pay you? You didn't do what I asked."

His tone hardened. "Don't back out on me, old woman. I said I'd try and that's what I expect to be paid for."

"I'm not—"

Wallace pursed his lips. "Do you want me to tell your son about our little bargain?"

Silence greeted his comment, and then Frieda sighed, resigned. "Fine, I'll wire the money."

"Nice doing business with you." Wallace closed his cell phone and tapped his steering wheel, pleased with his new strategy. He'd get money from Frieda but he knew his new cash flow was just getting started.

Rick was silent on the drive home and throughout dinner. Although it was a big feast, he couldn't focus. He still couldn't believe that Suzanne had married him. Despite all the things the judge and Hannah said, she'd stood up for him and Luke. It was as if they really meant something to her. But he decided he wouldn't make too much of it. She needed his money—that was probably what she was fighting for. But all the same, she belonged to him now. She was a Gordon. However, she didn't appear too pleased with that change and he didn't blame her. This special day seemed to be everything but. Not only the incident with the judge and Hannah, but Lyon showing up when he did. Now the dinner.

He looked at the food on his and Suzanne's plates. He'd told Mandy to handle the dinner arrangements with the chef and she'd gotten the order entirely wrong. He'd wanted to impress Suzanne by preparing an authentic French meal so that she'd know she'd married well, but he should have stuck with Southern fare because the chef couldn't tell the difference between au gratin and gravy. And Suzanne was allergic to nuts, but Mandy had ordered a banana nut cream-filled wedding cake. It was not the kind of wedding day he'd hoped for. He didn't even want to imagine what their wedding night would be like.

"I'm sorry, but we don't allow smoking in the house," he heard Suzanne say.

He looked up and saw his mother ready to light her cigarette.

"Well, the rules have changed, honey," Frieda said.

His mother had refused to attend the ceremony, but at least she'd come for dinner. She hadn't dressed up, but she had pulled her wig back into a ponytail. Rick shook his head. "No, Momma, she's right. If you want to smoke, you have to go outside."

His mother looked at him with the lighter carrying its flame. She put it closer to her cigarette.

"And if you light that now you might as well leave."

She glared at him, clicking the lighter closed. "You're going to take her side over mine?"

"It's not about taking sides, it's house rules."

"It wasn't a rule before."

"It's a rule now."

Suzanne spoke up, trying to ease the tension. "I just don't want Luke exposed to secondhand smoke."

Frieda glanced at the boy. "Think it will kill him on the spot?"

"It's not good for him or anyone."

"I don't need a lecture, honey. I've been smoking for years and I'm still alive and healthy."

Suzanne nodded, feeling it was best not to argue. "Yes," she said then looked down and screamed.

Rick jumped to his feet. "What is it?"

"Nothing," she said quickly. "I was just surprised."

"By what?"

"Luke's gift." She lifted the frog from her lap before it could hop away.

"His name is Harmon, Momma," Luke stated proudly, appearing from under the table. "I caught him for you."

"Thank you, dear, but let's return it to where you found it, okay?" She stood and Rick saw a large muddy smear on her white dress.

"Luke, you ruined her dress," Mandy scolded. "I told you to put it in a box."

"But he fit in my pocket," Luke protested.

"I'm sure he did," Suzanne said, "but if we're going to keep him he needs a proper shelter."

"He has our house."

"Our house isn't right for a frog. Let's go make him a place to stay so you can take care of him for me."

"Okay."

"But your dress," Mandy said, alarmed.

"It will wash," Suzanne said, looking at Luke again. "It's a lovely, thoughtful gift and later I'll teach you about when it's appropriate to give such gifts. Okay?"

Luke nodded.

Suzanne pushed in her chair. "Excuse us." They hurried out the room.

Frieda lifted her cigarette again. "Ever the fine lady of the house."

"I wasn't kidding about the smoking, Momma."

His mother scowled and shoved the lighter and cigarette into her handbag. "I hope you don't become too proud." She gestured to the table. "How much did you spend on this mush, anyway? A bunch of fancy stuff no one can pronounce."

He looked at her empty plate. "I didn't hear you complaining while you were shoveling mush into your mouth."

"I was hungry."

"I think the word is *ravenous*."

"No need to use big words you can't spell. At least I had an appetite. Your beloved bride hardly touched any of hers. I guess her tastes are more expensive."

"She doesn't like certain fish, such as tuna."

"Rick, I'm so sorry," Mandy said in an anxious voice. "I thought—"

"It's okay. You can start clearing the table."

Suzanne returned with Luke. "I think it's time for Luke's bed so I'll take him up. Thanks for a wonderful dinner, Mandy, and it was a pleasure seeing you, Mrs. Gordon." She smiled and left.

"She lies like a true Rand," Frieda grumbled, watching her go.

Rick fought to cut his soggy asparagus. "You mean a Gordon."

She swore then stood. "I need a smoke. Keep me company."

Rick sighed and joined his mother out on the porch. He stared at her. So many times he wondered why he loved this woman, but he always knew the answer. They were both survivors. She could be nasty or filthy at times, but he remembered her caring for him when no one else did. She'd prevented many blows from his father by diverting his attention with extra beer, food or something more. She was the one woman who stayed by his side through it all. He watched her light her cigarette then take a long drag. He watched the smoke drift up to the night sky. "You can still get yourself out of this," she said.

He groaned, not wanting to argue with her. "I don't want to."

"I hope you're not expecting a wedding night from that cold fish. It's going to take a lot more than a house and money to warm her up."

"What are you afraid of?"

She paused. "I don't know what you're talking about."

"I'm the one married to her, but you're the one concerned. Why? It's not like you to worry about me."

"I'm just speaking my mind."

"Well you can stop. It's a done deal."

Frieda pointed her cigarette at him. "Don't say I didn't warn you. But I'll tell you one thing, I'll put up with having to smoke on the porch, but I won't have her treating me like a second-class citizen. I'm your momma and you let her remember that. I'm the first Mrs. Gordon and she's the second. Just tell me one thing. What happens when she finds out the truth? That all this was revenge. That you orchestrated her father's ruin?"

Rick balled his hands into fists. He didn't want to think about it, but he had to. His mother was right. Every step he'd made over the past several years had been about revenge. He'd watched Gerald Rand's every move through a private detective agency he'd hired and he'd plotted and planned on the best way to destroy him. Then one day an opportunity came to him. Rand had pursued a partnership with a colleague and when their business venture hit a weak moment, Rick had enough money to go in for the kill and he'd slaughtered them. Rick hadn't felt guilty. Besides, if he hadn't someone else would have. He hadn't been touched by the rumors of Rand's desperate attempts to save his business or his ultimate demise, he'd only wanted vengeance. He was single focused. He would destroy the man and then get what he wanted: Rand's house and his daughter.

But meeting Suzanne again had altered the ferocity of his revenge, and he wanted her in his life for a completely different reason. One he still wouldn't allow himself to admit.

A malicious smile touched Frieda's lips. "You hadn't thought about that."

He nearly asked for a cigarette, but flexed his hands instead. "I'll take care of it."

"You'd better or you're going to fall through that big hole in your plan." She finished her cigarette and left.

Mandy disappeared upstairs and Rick sat in the living room alone. He waited for Suzanne to come back down after putting Luke to bed, but after another hour passed he decided to see what she was up to. Was she already in bed? She might not want to make love, but she'd learn that she wasn't going to be sleeping alone.

He walked up the stairs but stopped. This would be his first night in the house, and he didn't even know which bedroom was his. Between the wedding, moving and his business he hadn't paid attention to how Suzanne had set everything up. He knew where Luke's room was and checked on him. He walked over to the bed and pulled the sheets up closer. A fierce, protective love seized him every time he saw his son asleep. He tenderly stroked the boy's cheek, determined that everything would be different for his son than it had been for him. The sound of Luke's laughter or the sight of his smile filled Rick with pride and at times reminded him of a time he'd had that kind of joy so long ago with a woman who'd made him feel he could conquer the world. But that hadn't lasted and now that joy seemed false and hollow.

He gently closed the door and looked around. He knew Mandy was sleeping in a guest room downstairs but there were four other doors to enter and he didn't know which one was his. He knew the master bedroom was at the end of the hall, but was Suzanne there? Or was she in her old room? He let out a heavy sigh and went toward it. If she wasn't there, he'd find her.

He opened the door to the master bedroom then stopped. Candles covered nearly every surface and pink, white and red rose petals lay scattered on the carpet. But what captured his interest most was the woman on the bed, her beautiful brown body encased in a lace white-and-red teddy. She turned to him and smiled with an invitation that made his entire body go hard. "Hello, Rick," she said. "You promised me a passion-filled marriage. Well, tonight's your chance to prove it."

Chapter 14

Suzanne knew she'd offered Rick a challenge, but she didn't expect his response. However, he remained unpredictable. When she expected him to be cool, he was hot; when she expected him to be fast, he was slow. As she lay there watching him, she'd expected a cool reply, a devilish smile or a slow seductive look. He liked to take his time, cherish his control over a situation or a woman. And he definitely had the upper hand. He could reject her as he had before. She had taken a gamble and was fully aware that she could lose again.

But she didn't lose and Rick wasn't slow or calculating. One moment he was standing in the doorway, and the next his hot, wet mouth covered hers like hot fudge over ice cream. The touch of his lips shattered her completely, filling her with an insatiable hunger for him. She'd dared him to show her passion—but what he was delivering was much more. He expertly removed her teddy and caressed her breasts and then her thighs.

"You're beautiful."

She unbuttoned his shirt. "Let me see how beautiful you are."

He removed his clothes and brought her to him—his flesh meeting hers, releasing a sense of untamed, primitive emotions. Soon he was between her thighs, sending tingles of ecstasy through her that escalated to a moment of explosive pleasure.

"Hold me closer," he whispered.

"I am."

"Tighter. Like you'll never let me go."

"You think I might?" she teased.

"Dammit it wasn't supposed to be like this," he grumbled.

"Like what?"

For a moment his smoldering glance met hers, then he kissed her again, erasing the question from her mind. She'd made love to him before but she didn't remember it like this. As her hands cascaded over the muscles of his back she didn't feel the soft, supple flesh of a boy barely out of his teens, but that of a man. And it was a man who held her—but not just any man: her husband.

She caressed the inside of his leg with her foot. "I'm already enjoying the benefits of being your wife."

Rick briefly paused, feeling the impact of those words and what they symbolized. *Your wife.* She was his wife, they were now bound together by the laws of God and man. He'd been married before, but it hadn't felt like this. This wasn't how he'd planned it, but he could no longer deny how much he'd wanted this moment. At last she wasn't another man's wife. She was his. Something that had started as a farce—a marriage of convenience—felt real.

He held her tightly in his arms, almost afraid that she would disappear.

"God forgive me," he said in a hoarse whisper. "I won't let her go."

"Rick, is something wrong?"

Suddenly everything seemed wrong—his vengeance, his betrayal, his lies. "I didn't think it would be like this."

"Me, neither."

But Rick knew Suzanne didn't know what he meant. All those years ago they'd had sex and he'd expected it to be the same now, but somehow it meant more. Much more. They were more mature now and theirs wasn't the hot, frenzied lovemaking of passionate youths. He wanted to possess every inch of her—her scent intoxicated him, her full breasts filled him with desire and the sacred place between her thighs was his haven. He wanted to please her and let her know that she belonged to him. But he didn't expect to want to belong to her. He'd never cared about belonging to anyone. He'd prided himself on being his own man and never being tied down.

Rick squeezed his eyes shut, wanting to ask her why she'd thrown him aside all those years ago. But he wouldn't let himself be that vulnerable. His memory of that young girl didn't coincide with the woman beside him now. The woman who accepted his son without question.

"Something's wrong," she said.

He opened his eyes. "I just wish—"

She pressed her fingers against his mouth. "The past can't be changed. We only have now."

As he gathered her close, Rick knew that God may forgive him for all the wrong he'd done, but Suzanne never would once she knew the truth.

Suzanne soon fell asleep and Rick pulled the covers up to keep her warm, then he stared at the ceiling as the moon cast shadows on the wall.

He couldn't let himself succumb to her charms again. He had to keep his distance or this marriage wouldn't work. Only a weak man let himself be ruled by emotions and he was far from weak. He had to remember who Suzanne really was. What she was capable of. How could he let himself forget their last meeting when she'd met him outside the hardware store? For a second he'd let himself hope that she was going to say that she'd told her father to leave them alone and that she loved him. She hadn't even tried to talk to him in order to give him a chance to banish her father's words from his mind. That she was "using him just because she was frightened." That "she didn't know her own mind and would never run off with him." Instead she'd offered excuses he didn't want to hear. It was only days later when she started planning her wedding. He knew that Suzanne could blow hot and cold and he'd be ready for when the ice princess returned.

But she didn't. Over the following weeks Rick watched Suzanne, waiting for her to change back to the Suzanne he thought he knew: the arrogant Rand who put manners and pride before everything else. Instead she amazed him with her tenderness toward Luke, her patience with Mandy, who did the housekeeping while Suzanne looked after Luke as she contacted different nanny agencies. Rick was particularly interested. "They all sound good," he said, looking at their bios.

"They're meant to, but we can't just hire anyone. I had a nanny who was a fussy woman and always made me climb the stairs on the tips of my toes." Suzanne raised her voice to mimic that of her former nanny. "On the toes, dear, it helps your balance and is great for the calves." Rick laughed and Suzanne returned her voice to normal. "I want someone firm but kind for Luke."

And after six interviews she found Mrs. Perigene, a classy woman who'd been a professional nanny for many years. Rick was pleased with Suzanne's choice and so was Luke. When Mandy gave notice that she wanted to pursue another career, Rick decided to rehire Neena, Suzanne's old housekeeper. Upon hearing the news, Suzanne squealed with delight like a little girl.

"Neena!" she screamed when she saw the older woman at the door.

"I'm back, sugar."

The two women hugged, then Suzanne turned to him and flew into his arms and kissed him as if he'd offered her a trunkful of treasure. She looked up at him and blinked back tears. "You don't know how much this means to me. She was a very important person in my life. Like a mother. Thank you."

"You're welcome."

Neena took her hand. "You can thank him a lot more later. Now come and tell me all you've been up to. Are you working on a new book…?" she asked as they walked away.

Days later Suzanne surprised him when he came home and saw a strange man in his study. "Rick this is Mr. Matyn, your tailor."

"My what?"

"Your tailor."

"I don't need a tailor. I have plenty of clothes."

"You have two suits. I know, I've been in your closet and the rest of your clothes are too casual for a man in your position. I know you've been running your business your own way," she quickly said before he could protest. "But this is Anadale and appearance matters. Tim will help you dress more appropriately. Trust me."

Rick looked at the man with a measuring tape then Suzanne's determined expression, and knew he was a lost man. She was right. Even his colleagues noticed and appreciated his more sophisticated look and he felt good. Things got better from there. Suzanne brought down her violin and played for them in the evenings and he promised to buy Luke a piano so that he could learn to play.

As Suzanne continued to make their house a home, the more Rick couldn't keep his hands off her. He brushed her cheek as she worked on her book, rested against her as they watched TV, wrapped his arms around her waist in the kitchen, stole kisses on the porch, and in the bedroom nothing was off-limits.

Soon he was *almost* convinced that their marriage was real. That Suzanne truly was his. But he couldn't believe that yet. And he knew what he needed to do to remind himself that she wasn't his. One night he slipped out of bed and went into the living room. He pulled *Beneath the Ashes* from the bookshelf and nodded. It was time to find out the truth.

Frieda was finishing her breakfast of fried eggs, hash browns and bacon when someone pounded on the front door.

"I'm coming," she shouted. "No need to break the door down." When she opened it, she frowned. "Rick, did you lose your key?"

He held up the book, rage in his eyes. "You lied to me."

Frieda cast a nervous look at the novel in his hand and licked her lips. "I don't know what you're talking about."

"I read it."

"So?"

"There's nothing shameful or bad or cruel about us in there."

She lowered her gaze.

"What other lies have you told me?"

"Do you want a drink?" She turned toward the kitchen.

"Answer my question. What other lies are there?"

"I didn't lie."

He entered the house and slammed the door behind him. "Did Gerald Rand force himself on you?"

She spun around. "He might as well have. He told me he'd take care of me, and then when I gave him what he wanted, he treated me like a whore. The Rands deserve everything they got."

"I destroyed an innocent man because of what you told me. I believed you."

"Gerald Rand was far from innocent. He ruined my life and yours, too. He was a womanizer, a gambler and a liar."

"At least you have the lying in common." He sneered. "You let me believe—"

"Because you wanted to. Don't put all of the blame on me. When you were demolishing his company you were thinking about how the Rands ruled this town and you can't deny how Suzanne treated you. I was trying to protect you. I didn't want you to be treated the way Gerald treated me. That's exactly what she was doing. You hated her and him and that's what made you do what you did. He put your brother in prison. Remember? His daughter treated you like dirt. You wanted revenge as much as I did. I stoked a fire that was already burning and now you're falling for her crap again. Just because Suzanne's making your kid happy and keeping your bed warm doesn't mean she's changed."

Rick glanced away. "You don't know her like I do."

"I know her better than you do. I remember her mother and her aunt Bertha. Cool, calculating women who got their way through charm and manipulation."

"Suzanne is not like that."

"She's a Rand."

"She's different." He tapped the book. "She wrote about us, about me as though I mattered to her. As though she truly cared."

"She cared about selling books. She's devious. You should have seen how she tried to trick me when she came by looking for you."

Rick stilled. "When?"

Frieda hesitated, realizing she'd said something she shouldn't have. "It was a long time ago."

"She came by the house?"

Frieda began to turn. "I need a smoke."

Rick grabbed her shoulders and stopped her. "Did she come by the house?"

"Yes," she reluctantly admitted. "A couple of times she said she wanted to see you."

"And you never told me," he said, hurt clear in his voice.

"I was protecting you. Her father had said enough. What could she say?"

Rick stepped away from her as if she were a stranger. "We'll never know."

Frieda reached for him but stopped. "You were better off without her. Do you think you would have become the success you are if she'd stayed in your life? I know I did the right thing for you."

His shoulders drooped with despair. "All those years I wasted hating her. And now—"

"And now you have to be strong. It's too late."

"What is?"

She softened her tone. "It won't work. You've built your marriage on a rotten foundation and its only option is to crumble. You can't save it."

A bitter smile touched his lips. "I didn't make her sign a prenup."

Frieda swore. "You fool! Do you know what that means? She's already got money from her book and now she can leave and get more money?"

Rick met her gaze, glad that she didn't know about Suzanne's finances. "Yes. Whether she stays married to me or not she'll be a rich woman."

"And that's what she's counting on. If you think you

mean anything to her you're wrong. All you have to do is ask Wallace how much she took him for. Once she's done with you, we'll have nothing left."

"We?"

"I mean you," she stammered.

"Is that what you're afraid of? That she'll take what you think is yours."

"You're my son. What's yours is mine."

"Yes, and I'll always take care of you. There's nothing to worry about. Suzanne will never know. I made sure that nothing traces directly back to me."

Frieda opened her mouth then closed it.

Rick frowned. "You're not telling me something."

"I wanted you to be safe," she said helplessly.

"What have you done?"

"I told Wallace."

His gaze sharpened. "Everything?"

"Most of it. I wanted him to keep Suzanne away from you."

Rick pressed his fists to his eyes. "Momma."

"I was looking out for you."

He glared at her. "By ruining everything?"

"Please see things from my point of view."

"I have and that's been my problem," he snapped. He watched his mother's eyes fill with tears and softened his tone. "Don't cry. I'll handle this," he said, leaving.

Rick didn't go straight home. *Lyon knew.* He could destroy his whole charade. That explained his smugness at the courthouse. So far he'd been silent, but Rick knew he wouldn't be for long. He drove around for a while trying to figure out what his next move should be. He stopped at a bar not knowing what to do with himself.

He no longer smoked, or drank and other women were out of the question. He ordered a soda, ignoring the bartender's strange look.

"I didn't expect to see you here," Hannah said, sliding into the seat next to him. "Guess you haven't changed as much as people think."

"Not now, Hannah."

"You said you'd never marry."

"I meant it when I said it back then."

"I waited for you."

"You shouldn't have."

"Because you wanted a bigger target?"

He took a long swallow of his drink.

She caressed the curls on the back of his neck. "That's all right with me. I don't mind being the other woman."

He moved away from her. "One is enough for me."

"We were discreet before and no one will know."

He stood. "No. I promised Suzanne."

Hannah laughed. "We'll see how long that promise lasts."

Rick left the bar and aimlessly drove around. But after an hour he decided to go home. The moment he entered the house, the smell of wood polish, daffodils and banana muffins greeted him. No stale cigarette smoke or old laundry. This was his house—no, his home. He peeked into the family room and saw Suzanne typing on her laptop and Luke lying on the carpet near her, with his frog Harmon by his side, coloring.

Rick gripped the door frame. He now had what he wanted and he could lose it all in a moment, and he had no one to blame but himself.

Rick began to step back before he was seen, but Luke lifted his head. "Daddy," he said with joy, and then he ran up and hugged him.

"Hello."

Suzanne put her laptop aside and came up to him. "How was your day?"

"Busy." Although she raised her mouth to him, he kissed her on the cheek and turned away, not seeing her worried look. "What's for dinner?"

"Ribs I think."

"Good." He nodded and headed to their bedroom, walking away from the life he didn't deserve.

Chapter 15

Something was wrong. Suzanne stared at Rick with growing concern as he ate his dinner. Over the past few days he'd been distant. What had gone wrong? She tried her best to make everything work. She kept the house clean and his food was always ready. She performed the role her mother had, but somehow it didn't seem to be enough even though she'd dived into her role as mother to his son with everything she had. She scheduled numerous activities with Luke, both alone and with Rick. One of the first places they went to was Hershey Park, in Pennsylvania.

As a child, Suzanne had always wanted to visit the park, but her parents didn't approve of theme parks. Now, with an eager little boy and a willing dad, they scheduled a three-day visit to the park. This was followed by several trips to the local zoo, the national aquarium and the local botanical garden. But two of Luke's favorite places to visit were story time at the local library and Saturday morning theater at the downtown repertory theater. Suzanne was amazed by how thrilled Luke was to see and discover things. His entire face lit up when watching the actors, and at bedtime he forced Suzanne to reread the stories he heard at the library. Motherhood felt right. She loved answering his questions. She loved being there for him. She loved, that each morning he greeted the day with excitement. Needless to say, getting him to go to bed at night was usually a struggle. Up until he said his prayers, and was tucked into bed, he kept talking about what he had done that day. But not all nights had been easy.

"Why not?" Luke demanded when she wouldn't allow him to take Harmon to bed with him.

"Because I said so."

Luke screamed and cried until Rick entered the room. "What's going on here?"

Luke ran up to his father and pointed at Suzanne. "I want a new momma."

Rick covered his mouth to keep from smiling and made sure not to catch Suzanne's eye. He cleared his throat. "Why?"

"Because she won't let me sleep with Harmon."

"Then you can't."

"But I want to."

"You can't always do what you want. And you'd better learn to mind your momma because she's the only one you get."

Luke scrunched up his face. Rick lightly swatted

him on the bottom. "Stop being a brat and go to bed or I may not let you have any of these animals in your room."

Luke quickly fixed his face and jumped into bed. "I'll be good now, but I'm still angry."

"That's all right," Suzanne said, tucking him in. "As long as you go to sleep."

"I'm going to stay up all night."

Suzanne straightened. "As long as you don't leave your bed, that's fine. Good night."

He yawned. " 'Night."

Rick kissed his son on the forehead and followed Suzanne out of the room. "Sorry about that," he said.

"Don't be, he's just being a kid. Thanks for backing me up."

He rested an arm around her shoulders. "We're a team, but I don't want you doing too much. You can let the nanny give him his baths and put him to bed."

"I don't mind. I love being with him."

At first Rick was silent as they walked down the hall, then he said in a quiet voice, "I'm glad. He's taught me patience. Before I had him I was impulsive, reckless and selfish, but the moment I held him I wanted to be a different man."

"And you've succeeded," she said when they reached the stairs.

"Mostly," Rick said, walking down.

Suzanne snapped her fingers. "We have to do a portrait."

He turned to her. "A what?"

"A family photo." When he continued to look blank

she shook her head. "You've never done a family photo before?"

"No."

"Not even when you were a kid?"

"You've met my momma, right? And besides her, we'd have to schedule a day when my father was sober."

"Sorry."

"Don't be," he said, continuing down the stairs. "Let's do it."

Their family portrait now hung over the fireplace and was the perfect image of happiness, but she knew it was a lie. Rick was pleased with her as a mother for his son, but as a wife she felt as though she was failing. And balancing the new roles hadn't been easy. Her writing schedule was totally off. As a single woman her schedule had been flexible, she could devote an entire day to her work, but being a mother and wife changed that.

There was the day she planned to spend the morning working on her manuscript when Luke woke up with a slight temperature and she found herself spending the entire morning in the doctor's office. Then there was the time she was working in the living room only to discover that Luke kept making so much noise outside that she couldn't concentrate. Eventually, she discovered that her best times to work were getting up an hour earlier in the morning, and grabbing an hour after she put Luke to bed, before joining Rick.

But being parents hadn't brought them any closer together and Suzanne wondered if she'd entered another relationship where what she did wasn't enough. Was this what he'd expected from their marriage? That they would live separate lives? Yes, he was a passionate lover, but sometimes she just wanted to sit and talk and find out about his day and tell him about hers. She didn't just want a physical connection, she wanted an emotional one.

She'd tried to develop one by taking down the violin from the attic. It had been one of the hardest things for her to do—reminding her of the times she'd played for him and of Melba's strict but gentle teaching. "Let the music sing through you," she used to say. "Let it speak what you cannot say." And one night with Luke and Rick gathered in the family room she played for them, letting the instrument in her hands say what she was afraid to. That she loved them and would forever. But although her performance hadn't changed anything between them, Suzanne soon found comfort in it and after dinner she would sit on the porch and play.

"That sounded sad," Neena said one evening after Suzanne had finished a somber piece.

Suzanne put her violin in its case. "It is."

"Your mother used to love hearing you play."

"But she forced me to practice in the attic."

"She would leave the door open and listen, it gave her joy."

The thought of her mother caused Suzanne pain. She'd been a disappointment. Her mother had tried to convince her to stay with Wallace, but she'd ignored her and become an embarrassment. She'd left Wallace and Anadale searching for a happiness that didn't exist.

"I read your book. It was wonderful and so uplifting. I liked the end."

Suzanne snapped the violin case closed. "Me, too. But happy endings only appear in fiction. My mother wasn't happy, Melba wasn't happy and I'm—" She sighed with frustration. "I made a mistake. I shouldn't have married him."

"Shh," Neena said and Suzanne didn't understand her harsh censure until she saw Rick standing in the door.

She sat, paralyzed. She couldn't read his expression so she didn't know how much he'd heard. "I just came to say that there's a movie on you might like," he said.

"Rick, I didn't mean it."

"Didn't mean what?" he said with innocence, but his gaze was too sharp to match his tone. He had heard her words, but he didn't want to discuss it and she wouldn't force him.

"I'll be right in."

After he'd gone back inside, Suzanne felt a wave of guilt and many times tried to let him know how happy she was but that hadn't mattered, and now as she sat across from him at the table she knew she could no longer take his silence. She decided she wouldn't go on guessing what was wrong, she'd make him tell her. That night as they prepared for bed she confronted him. "What's wrong?"

"Work has been stressful."

"Are you worried about money?" Suzanne asked as she pulled on her nightdress.

He sent her a cool glance. "Are you?"

"Only if you are."

"I'm not," he sighed. "There's plenty of money."

"Because if there wasn't I'm okay."

"What do you mean?"

"I received a movie option for my book and I sent in

my manuscript last week so I'll get the rest of my advance. I also have another publisher wooing me to write for them."

"I'm happy for you, but money's not a problem."

"Have people been harassing you in town?"

"No."

"Are you unwell?"

"No."

"Are you—"

He threw up his hands in exasperation. "Why are you asking me all these questions?"

"Because I want to know what's wrong."

"Nothing is wrong."

She bit her lip. "I know you heard what I said that night on the porch, but I didn't mean it. I was just having a bad day. I don't regret marrying you."

"Yet," he mumbled, pulling back the bedsheets.

Suzanne reached out and clutched his hand. "Haven't I done what you wanted?" she said with a note of desperation. "Isn't it enough? If it's not, please tell me."

He gently smoothed down her hair and said in a tender voice she hadn't heard in weeks, "You're everything I wanted."

"Then what's wrong?"

His eyes flashed with impatience. "Stop asking me that."

"I can't help it. You're not acting like yourself. You don't seem comfortable here."

He slipped into bed and pulled up the sheets. "I never said—"

She went to the other side of the bed and got in, as well. "You don't have to say it, I can sense it. You act like you're visiting or a guest. You don't act as though this is your permanent home." She drew her knees up to her chest. "I know it's hard to take over this place, but I think I have a solution."

He groaned. "I'm afraid to ask."

"It's summer and every year my family used to throw a party. I think we should. That way people can get to know you."

"You mean see me as respectable?"

Suzanne frowned. "If you don't like the idea just say so."

Rick paused. "Go ahead. Let them satisfy their curiosity," he said, resigned.

Suzanne bit her lip. "I just want you to be happy."

He wrapped an arm around her waist, drawing her close, and kissed her lightly on the mouth. "I am happy. It's just that happiness for me doesn't last."

"It will this time."

He turned away. "So who are we going to invite to this party?"

Suzanne sighed, knowing the other topic was closed, so she decided to paint the picture he wanted to see. "Oh, all the key influential people and there will be flowers and a band…"

Several weeks later Suzanne shifted through the mail, stunned. None of the RSVPs had come back. Something strange was going on and she knew the one person who could tell her why. She called Della. Della was the hot spot to knowing the gossip about town. If it were a paying job, she'd be a millionaire. When Della picked up the phone Suzanne described the situation. "And no one has replied yet."

"I know." She groaned. "Everyone knows about your party but most are afraid to go. You have two things against you. You've barely been in town or talked to anyone since your return. You've ignored requests for interviews by the local press, and when you were briefly in town you insulted Hannah."

"That's more than two things and I did not insult Hannah."

"That's not the story she's spreading, which brings me to our second problem."

Suzanne rolled her eyes, not in the mood to correct her. "What is it?"

"You mean aside from the fact that you married Rick Gordon?"

"Yes."

"It's your book or rather your career. You're a novelist. People are afraid they'll show up in your next novel. Now that's not necessarily a bad thing if you put the right spin on it. Why don't you write a glowing short story about the town and post it on your Web site and offer it for free. Also give a copy to the paper. Then do everything locally. Get your nails done in town, buy from Lanie's Boutique and visit the Ladies League. You need to be seen."

Suzanne groaned. "I hate the Ladies League."

"Me, too, but you have to answer one major question. Do you love this town or not? Your answer will determine whether people attend your party or not."

Suzanne thanked her then hung up the phone. Della was right. If she was going to be an Anadale resident she had to act like one. She had to fall in love with the town again. She had to fall in love with the historic town whose strength of character seemed to improve with age—the brick stone walkways, grand old homes and quaint numerous bed-and-breakfasts. She had to admire how the summer brought thousands of fireflies and the scent of the ocean.

The next day Suzanne traded in her flashy sports car for a more subdued brand. She bought two dresses at Lanie's Boutique and spent an afternoon drinking tea at the Ladies League. She visited Luke's school where he would attend in the fall, and introduced herself to the administration, and also spoke to the local bank president and discussed giving them her business. Instead of rushing down Main Street, Suzanne walked at a leisurely pace and didn't mind the stares and whispers as she passed. When she went into the local grocery store she overheard two women talking, Suzanne recognized them as the mayor's wife and sister.

"Oh, there she is Suzanne Rand," the mayor's wife said in a low voice, as though she didn't want to be noticed.

"You mean Gordon," the other woman corrected.

"Right, if her father was alive…"

"I'm not surprised. She's not really lucky when it comes to men."

Suzanne turned to the pair unable to listen anymore. "Yes, you're right and thanks to you I've got a great idea for a new book. It will be about a woman unlucky in love. I'll dedicate it to you. What do you think?"

At first the women stared at her speechless then the thought of being mentioned in a book had them talking. Suzanne left them feeling as though they had contributed to the creation of the next blockbuster.

After that the responses flooded in and Suzanne

found herself hosting a boisterous garden party. It was a grand catered affair. She looked stunning in a turquoise off-the-shoulder sheath dress, with her hair upswept, and a pair of studded diamond earrings. She stared out on the landscaped lawn and canopy, while the music from a band from Charlotte played and the scent of the sumptuous catered feast filled the air. Chinese lanterns hung from the trees as solar-powered spotlights provided extra lighting. Suzanne greeted each of her guests, remembering the gatherings of the past, except now she was the lady of the house and a Gordon, not a Rand. Thankfully, everything was going well. Rick seemed to move easily among the crowd and everyone appeared to be enjoying themselves.

Pleased with the party's success, Suzanne disappeared into the house and went upstairs to check on Luke. She knew the party atmosphere would be too much for him, so she'd instructed his new nanny to watch after him in his room. When she peeked in, he looked happy playing with his amphibian friend Harmon, then Suzanne went to her bedroom to touch up her makeup. She was applying her lipstick when a figure came up behind her and placed a kiss on the back of her neck.

"Hmm, that's nice," she said.

He kissed lower.

"That's nice, too."

"Can I keep going?" Rick said in a velvet smooth voice.

"There are guests downstairs."

"Then try to be quiet."

Suzanne turned to him. "I'm always quiet."

He lifted a brow.

Her cheeks grew warm. "Most times."

He reached for her. "Then make sure this is one of those times."

She nudged him and stood. "We have guests who want to see us."

"You mean me," he grumbled. "I feel like I'm on display."

"Well, you're passing with flying colors."

Rick stood and took her hand. "Only because you're making me look good. You've done an amazing job with this party."

"You deserve it."

He kissed her, but before he could deepen the kiss Suzanne pulled away. "Someone could come in and find us."

He drew her close again and whispered against her lips. "No one would dare come upstairs."

"We shouldn't be doing this now. We have an obligation to our guests."

He removed one strap of her dress. "I'm feeling vulnerable right now. I need you to build up my morale."

"Your morale appears intact to me," Suzanne said, feeling the evidence of his desire.

He removed her other strap then unzipped the back of her dress. "I'd hate to see it falter."

She folded her arms to keep her dress up. "I've never done something like this."

He coaxed her to unfold one arm. "Yes, you have."

"Not with guests downstairs and eating outside on our lawn."

"That's okay." He unfolded her other arm and watched the dress fall. "Let's start a new Gordon tradition."

Twenty minutes later Suzanne and Rick returned to the party. Nobody asked about their disappearance, although some probably hazarded a guess as to where they were and what they had been doing. Suzanne's face was flushed and Rick no longer had on his tie or belt. However, the party continued late into the evening without incident and Suzanne silently congratulated herself until she saw Rick talking to Wallace. They seemed to be talking in low voices. She marched over to them.

"Wallace, what are you doing here? You weren't invited."

He looked as handsome and devious as ever, dressed all in black. "I just figured you had overlooked sending my invitation. I forgive you."

"If you're here to cause trouble—"

He rested a hand on his chest as though she'd wounded him. "Now why would I do that? I just wanted to wish you both happiness."

"Next time just send a postcard." Suzanne grabbed Rick's arm. "Come, there's someone I want you to meet."

"Don't forget what I said, Gordon," Wallace called after them.

Once they were a good distance away, Suzanne asked, "What did he say?"

"A lot of things. Don't worry about it."

"Did he say something about me? What did he want?"

Rick cupped her face. "I don't want you to worry about it." He kissed her forehead. "Now we can't ignore our guests for a second time." He winked then walked away.

But Suzanne could not focus on her guests or the party.

She continued watching Wallace and Rick until she spotted Frieda dropping her cigarette ashes behind a bush.

"Well done," a female voice said behind her.

Suzanne spun around and saw Jean, who looked a lot less formidable than she had in the courthouse. "I'm trying."

"You succeeded. This is a fabulous party. Rick won't have as much trouble in town as he has had in the past. I've already heard two people say they want to do business with him and I encouraged them."

Suzanne knew the impact of the judge's endorsement. In the past no one from the upper echelon would do business with a Gordon, but that had changed. "Thank you."

"Don't thank me. Rick did it himself. He's worked himself up the hard way. That's something to be admired."

"I know."

"And your book isn't so bad, either."

"I thought you said—"

Jean shrugged. "It improved on a second reading. So when's the next one coming out?"

"I don't know. Hopefully next year."

She patted Suzanne on the back. "I look forward to reading it." Jean looked up at the house, glanced at Rick, and sighed. "I guess you knew what you were doing after all. Your father would still turn over in his grave, but you've gotten all that you wanted." She grabbed a drink from a passing waiter and walked off. Suzanne watched her leave wondering if that was true.

Suzanne questioned herself even more as summer turned into fall. Luke enrolled in school and although

Rick tried to be attentive she knew there was something else on his mind. He left home early and came back late. When she caught him talking in low tones on his cell phone one afternoon she knew she could no longer take his secrecy. Her first marriage had been filled with secrets. With people who called then hung up, the scent of perfume on Wallace's jackets that wasn't hers. There had been late nights, which couldn't be accounted for. Rick had promised he'd never cheat on her, but now she wasn't so sure, and she needed to find out the truth.

One cool autumn afternoon she told Mandy to briefly watch Luke because it was Mrs. Perigene's day off and she took him to play outside while Suzanne waited for Rick to come home. When he did she met him at the front door and said, "Who is she?"

He briefly kissed her on the cheek and walked past. "Who is who?"

The touch of his lips was warm and sweet and he looked exhausted, but Suzanne was determined to uncover the truth. "Are you seeing someone?"

"Am I supposed to be seeing someone?"

"Rick, I'm asking you a serious question. Is there another woman?"

He ran a tired hand down his face. "Why would I have another woman when I have you?"

"That hasn't stopped men before."

He rested his hands on her shoulders. "Suzanne, I told you I wouldn't cheat on you." He lowered his voice. "There is no other woman in my life except you. Please believe me."

Suzanne bit her lip, unsure.

"Please," he repeated with a note of sadness.

"Okay, but I know you're hiding something from me."

"It's for your own good." He pressed his fingers against her lips to keep her from talking. "I want you to promise me something."

"What?"

"Promise me that no matter what happens between us you won't take it out on Luke."

Suzanne stepped back and stared at him confusion. "What could happen?"

"Just promise me."

"Not until you tell me what is bothering you. Is it your mother?"

He frowned. "Why do you ask?"

"At the party you two were very tense around each other and you don't visit her as you used to. I don't want to pry, but it's like she has a strange hold on you."

He walked into the living room. "She's a damn noose around my neck and determined to remind me of my past. Every time I look at her I feel poor all over again." He leaned against the mantel. "I'm trying to move forward, but she won't. No matter how hard I try. Even after her ministroke that left her right hand a little weak, she didn't change."

"Maybe she's afraid of the future. But that's her problem not yours, the past is gone."

"No, unfortunately, the past still haunts me." Rick took her hand and led her to the couch. He sat down and sighed. "I'm not a good man. I'm what they've always said—a rotten no-good Gordon and I've done some bad things."

"So there is another woman."

"Suzanne," he said, exasperated, "there's no other woman."

"Then it can't be that bad," she said with relief. "You've stayed out of prison," she teased.

He didn't smile.

"Rick, I wouldn't have married you if I thought you were bad."

"You married me because you had no choice. You needed the money."

"No, that's not—"

A scream stopped her words. Mandy burst into the room with a lifeless Luke in her arms. "I found him in the pond."

Suzanne jumped to her feet, fear gripping her heart. "You were supposed to watch him."

"I *was* watching him," she cried. "I turned my back for one second."

"A second is enough." She grabbed Luke and rested him on the floor, ready to perform CPR. "Call 911," she ordered as she checked his vitals. Suzanne and Rick started the breaths and chest compressions and continued until the EMTs arrived and whisked Luke away in the ambulance. Suzanne and Rick drove close behind.

Chapter 16

Rick sat in the waiting room, staring at the stark walls, not seeing anything. Was this his punishment? If he lost Luke he'd lose the one thing that was truly his. His entire life had been filled with hand-me-downs—from his clothes to his reputation. But Luke had been new and pure and was a part of him. What would his life be like without him? His marriage was already a sham. He feared that Suzanne would have no reason to stay now. He wondered what would hold them together when she found out the truth. How would he convince her to stay?

"Rick?"

He turned and saw Suzanne, who'd disappeared into the restroom after they'd taken Luke into the emergency room. He rushed over to her and held her. "They got a pulse started. But they're not sure how he will do because they don't know how long he was in the water."

"I'm sure he'll be okay. He has to be."

"Yes," he said, desperate to believe her. He glanced up at the ceiling, then looked away and closed his eyes instead. There were no prayers he could offer. He'd gotten back at Rand for the years he'd treated his family like trash. He'd destroyed him and gotten his revenge, but in the end Rand had won. Cosmic justice had the last laugh. He opened his eyes when he heard hurried footsteps; soon his mother appeared in the doorway.

"How is he?" she asked in an anxious voice.

"It's touch and go."

"What does that mean?"

"It means they're not sure of anything."

Her voice trembled. "You mean he could die?"

"Yes," he snapped. "I'm surprised you care."

Suzanne stared at him, appalled. "Rick, that's not fair."

"Fair?" His voice cracked. "She never accepted Luke as her grandson. Now she doesn't have to." He turned and walked over to a window.

Suzanne turned to Frieda. "He's just upset. We all are, but I know that everything is going to be all right."

Frieda stared at Rick's back then Suzanne. "Spoken like a true Rand, as though you've got God on speed dial," she said bitterly. "I need a smoke." She left.

Suzanne stood, wondering who to comfort first. She looked at Rick but remembered the shimmer of tears in his mother's eyes and decided to follow her outside. She found Frieda huddled under a streetlight, the autumn wind blowing her thin coat.

Frieda turned when she heard Suzanne's footsteps.

"You have to get yourself nearly killed to find a decent place to smoke."

Suzanne took off her coat and put it on the older woman's shoulders.

"You don't need to be nice to me," she grumbled, pulling the coat tight about her.

"We're family."

"A costly booby prize," she scoffed.

"I don't think so. Mothers are important. Especially those who love their children and I know you love Rick."

"He blames me for his father, but I couldn't leave him." She sent Suzanne a sharp look. "And not every woman could do what Melba did. No matter how much they may want to."

"He knows that."

"I did my best."

"Yes, so did my mother before she died. I miss her."

Frieda inhaled then released. "She was a smart, classy woman, very different from me."

"No. She was also afraid of her husband, even though she loved him. I won't judge her and I won't judge you, if you won't do the same."

Frieda stared at her for a long moment, her gaze filling with new respect. "I've read your book back to front more than ten times. Rick once asked me why and I couldn't tell him, but I'm going to tell you." She took another drag of her cigarette, her hand slightly trembling. "It was like you took Melba's story and made it mine. So many times I thought about doing what she did or leaving him. The experts always tell you to do that, but I couldn't. I guess I couldn't believe

I'd made such a big mistake." Frieda studied her cigarette. "He wasn't always like that. In the beginning he wasn't so bad." A brief smile touched her mouth. "He could be charming and funny. It was the drinking that changed that and the bills and the layoffs. His drinking got real bad when Rick was born." She absently raised the cigarette to her lips. "I kept trying to remember him as he was." She sent Suzanne a curious glance and when the younger woman didn't say anything she felt free to reveal more. "Your book was filled with heartbreak and pain and love." She glanced up at the sky and blinked back tears. "Oh, the way Donna loved Roland always got to me." She looked at Suzanne. "I was jealous of you. Yes, jealous. See, Rick was all I had to cling to at the time. In my house I didn't have a lot of things, but Rick was mine. Then you came along and I was afraid I was going to lose him. His other flings never bothered me because those women came and went, but you were different. You should have seen him when he used to come home after seeing you. He couldn't stop smiling and nothing his father said or did bothered him. It was as though he used you as some sort of shield against the rottenness of our lives.

"I envied how happy you made him and I didn't want to be alone, so I had to keep you away. I'm not proud of that, but I did it and I kept him close by letting him share in my misery by feeding him my hatred." She dragged on her cigarette then exhaled. "I'm a bitter, ugly, old woman and I don't deserve your kindness." She started to remove the coat, but Suzanne stopped her.

"I forgive you. Let's forget about the past."

Frieda looked at her with amazement. "You understand me. I didn't think you would."

"I understand a lot of things."

"I can see that now. I didn't before. I guess I've been so busy thinking people were looking down on me, I didn't realize I was doing the same. Rick was right about you. You're good for him."

"Not without Luke. I can't have children and Rick only married me to take care of his son. Without Luke our marriage is nothing."

"But you told me that Luke's going to be okay and if you want me to believe it, you have to believe it, too." Frieda dropped her cigarette on the floor then crushed it under her shoe. "Let's go wait inside."

When the two women returned to the waiting room they saw that Rick hadn't moved from his spot. Suzanne told Frieda that she was going to get something to drink then left. Frieda looked at her son with a mixture of love and regret then walked over to him. "I was wrong about everything. I'm sorry. She's a good woman, even if she is a Rand, and I'm glad you're with her."

Rick folded his arms.

"And Luke means everything to me. I'm going to change my ways. I won't say anything bad about him again. I promise. It's just that this world isn't kind to the weak and—"

"You want him to be strong," Rick finished. "I know."

"I've just been so used to hatred and bitterness and cruel words that I didn't know how to be different. But I want things to be different from now on. Do you think we can start over?"

Rick was silent a moment and then held out his arm. She went to him and he held her close.

"Don't ever tell her the truth," Frieda said in a hurried whisper. "You need her. *We* need her."

"It's too late and you know that."

She gripped the front of his shirt. "It's not too late. Luke will pull through and you can leave this town and be far away from anyone who could find out."

"I'm not going anywhere. I'm going to take care of Wallace." He stared down at his mother. "But you should have told me about him first. I hate surprises."

"I thought he'd prove useful at the time. I was wrong and I admit it. You just have to keep him away from Suzanne."

"Don't worry about it. I'm—"

"Would you two like something to drink?" Suzanne said behind them.

Rick and his mother shared a look, and Rick took the cool drink from her. A half hour later they learned that Luke would fully recover. He spent the night in the hospital and was sent home the next day. Traumatized by the incident, Mandy returned to her family, and Frieda took over the role of caring for him on Mrs. Perigene's days off, and having nothing else to do she would also help Neena with household duties.

Early one morning, after Luke had gone off to school, Suzanne called Frieda into the kitchen.

"I hope your schedule is free for the next several hours."

"How come?" Frieda asked curiously.

"Because we're going to have a girls' day out," she announced.

Frieda made a face. "Oh, I don't think I'll be good

at that. I'm not much into that modern 'woman bonding' stuff."

"Female bonding," Suzanne corrected. "That's not what I'm talking about."

"What do you mean then?"

"Well, I've decided you need a makeover."

"Why?" Frieda said, insulted, touching her wig. "What's wrong with the way I look?"

"I'm not saying there's anything wrong with you, it's just that I think it's time you treated yourself. You don't need to worry, you won't come back looking like someone else. I just thought a day at the spa for a full-body massage and having your hair styled at the salon would be nice to do."

"But, I don't have much hair to style," Frieda admitted. "I'm not sure that—"

Suzanne took her hand, sensing the older woman's anxiety. "Come on, it'll be fun."

To Frieda's surprise, Suzanne had conspired with Della and made arrangements with Della's hairstylist, Robin, to fit Frieda with a more attractive wig, and to give her natural hair a needed haircut, so that she wouldn't have to wear a wig all the time. After the spa, where they had been treated to a stone massage, Suzanne and Frieda sat in The Modern Woman's Hair Salon.

Frieda was given the royal treatment and after going through a wide selection of wigs of different lengths and colors, Robin decided on a medium-length, dark brown wig, with red highlights. At first Frieda felt naked without her long hair, but once she saw the finished product she could hardly believe her eyes. Robin was an expert stylist and had shaped and cut the wig to frame Frieda's face. Both the color and shape highlighted her features and made her look ten years younger.

Next Suzanne took Frieda to a boutique she used to frequent and helped her select a new miniwardrobe. That afternoon Frieda decided to pick Luke up from school wearing a lovely, straight, knee-length green skirt and blue blouse instead of the jeans and T-shirt she frequented. Luke told her she looked pretty and when Rick saw his mother he laughed.

"I see that Suzanne got ahold of you," he said.

Frieda proudly turned around in a circle, so he could see the entire makeover. "Do you like it?"

"You look as beautiful as a queen."

Suzanne snapped her fingers as an idea struck her. "Wait a second," she said and dashed upstairs. Minutes later she came down with a crown and placed it on Frieda's head. "Now it's perfect."

Frieda touched the crown in awe. "Is this your Miss Anadale crown?"

"Yes."

"I can't wear this."

"Of course you can, Momma," Rick said. "You always wanted to."

"This is the happiest day of my life," she said, her voice trembling.

Rick took out his cell phone to take a picture. "Smile for me," he said. Then he snapped the picture of Luke and Suzanne smiling with Frieda wiping away tears of joy.

Everything seemed to settle back to normal until a

week later when Rick forgot his cell phone. Suzanne was working in the kitchen when she heard it ring. She was about to ignore it but decided to check out who was calling. When she saw the name she froze. Wallace Lyon. Why was Wallace calling Rick? She remembered the look Wallace had given Rick at the courthouse and the same sly expression had crossed his face at the party. What was he up to? She had a sinking feeling she knew.

Suzanne sent him a text message from Rick to meet at their house at seven. When he immediately replied, she smiled.

Chapter 17

Wallace bobbed his head in tune to the beat of his favorite song, which blared from his radio, as he drove to his meeting with Rick. At last Gordon was going to pay up. He knew he would eventually. The dirt he had on him was too good. He parked in the driveway, checked his image in the rearview mirror and straightened his jacket before running up the steps and ringing the doorbell.

He plastered on a smile when the door opened, but his smile disappeared when he saw Suzanne.

"What are you doing here?" he said.

"This is where I live."

He quickly recovered himself. "I'm here to see Gordon—uh, Rick."

"But you're not going to. You're going to see me." She opened the door wider. "Come in."

He hesitated. "What game are you playing?"

"The same game you are."

He narrowed his gaze. "How much do you know?"

"Enough to be interested, but I'm not having this conversation in the doorway." When she saw his nervous look, she said, "No one else is here except us."

Wallace entered and followed Suzanne into the living room. She sat and crossed her legs. "So this information you have. How much is it worth?"

"Why?"

"I might take you up on your offer of a book collaboration. You could have royalties coming in for years."

"It has to do with your husband."

"I don't care."

"And you."

She shrugged with nonchalance. "Even better. You know I always put my own spin on things."

Wallace leaned back, amazed. "So you *did* marry him for his money."

"What other reason could there be?"

"You're right. He's just a bastard Gordon. But he's fallen for you hard. You wouldn't believe how much he was willing to pay me."

"I can imagine. Blackmail can be lucrative."

He tugged on his collar, uncomfortable with the word. "I wouldn't call it blackmail."

"Why not? You've done it before. Everyone thinks I left you because of the women, but we both know the real reason."

"You shouldn't have left. My office was like a well-oiled machine when you were in charge. I got the clients and you kept them happy. We were a good team."

"We could be again."

"What made you change your mind?"

"New York softened some of my high ideals. So tell me what you know."

Wallace opened his mouth then stopped. "It won't be worth as much if I tell you. I'll have nothing over Gordon anymore. Sorry, honey. You're not getting me that cheap."

"That's okay. Getting you on tape is enough for me."

He paused. "What?"

"You heard me. I wonder what the police will think when I hand it over to them."

"You wouldn't." He sneered. "You didn't have guts enough then and you're bluffing now."

"Are you willing to risk it?"

Wallace began to smile. "You do love him. That's what this is all about." He shook his head in sympathy. "And you're just part of his game plan. He's using you."

"I thought you said he cared enough to spend—"

"I was lying to you. He's willing to pay because he doesn't want you leaving with half. But we can both end up winners in the end. You give me the tape and I'll tell you what I know."

"Fine." She removed her secret recorder. "Talk first."

"Not a chance."

"Then you won't get the tape."

He stood and walked over to her seat. "Oh, you'll give me the tape, Suzanne, whether you want to or not." He loomed over her and held out his hand.

She swallowed. "How do I know if I can trust you?"

"That's not my problem." He wiggled his fingers. "Don't taunt me, Suzanne. You know what happens when you do." He touched a faded scar under her jaw.

She turned her face away, disgusted by his touch. "I won't—"

His hand shot out and fastened itself around her neck. "Yes, you will." He forced her to her feet. "You didn't plan this very well, but you, like most people, underestimated me. Here you are all alone and there's nothing you can do about it."

Tears of pain stung her eyes and she fought to breathe through his tight hold. "If you leave a mark, Rick will know."

He squeezed tighter. "Rick doesn't care. I want the tape."

The look in her ex-husband's eyes chilled her. Wallace was ruthless and he'd demonstrated it many times in their marriage. And although she didn't want to believe his words about Rick, there was a faint kernel of truth. If Rick had cared about her, he would have told her about being blackmailed. But he'd preferred to pay to keep his secrets than trust her. However, she couldn't let Wallace win. She had started this game and she would finish it, no matter the price. She spat in his face.

He swore, but he didn't release his hold. "For that you're going to owe me a lot more than a tape." He brought his mouth down on hers with cruel possession. She struggled against him and bit his lip.

Wallace released her, reeling back in pain. Suzanne backed away, creating distance between them.

He laughed at her effort as he dabbed the blood on his lip. "You can't escape me, Suzanne. I know things and I know that Gordon—" He stopped with a sharp jerk then collapsed to the floor.

Suzanne stared at his fallen form in disbelief. When she looked up she saw Frieda with a tire iron in her hand.

"Are you all right?" Frieda said in a shaky tone.

"Yes." Suzanne's gaze fell on Wallace's still form and she saw blood seeping from his head. She broke through her paralysis and raced over to him. She dropped to her knees and frantically checked for a pulse.

"I saw his car," Frieda said, "so I came in around the back. I took Luke upstairs then came down to check on you and I couldn't believe what I saw. I knew I had to help you."

Suzanne snatched her hand back from Wallace's neck. "Frieda—"

"I put Luke upstairs," Frieda repeated, "so he's safe."

Suzanne slowly stood, wringing her hands. "Frieda."

"And now you're safe. I made sure."

"Frieda, he's dead."

Frieda dropped the tire iron and it clattered to the floor. She vigorously shook her head. "He can't be."

"He is."

"Oh, God."

Suzanne covered her mouth and stared at Wallace's body, not knowing what else to say.

Frieda spun to look out the window when she heard a car drive up. Headlights briefly flashed into the room. "Rick's home." Frieda rushed over to the body. "Help me hide him."

Suzanne blocked her. "We don't have time." She shook her head, annoyed by her irrational reply. "I mean we shouldn't."

"Then what are we going to do?"

They heard footsteps on the porch then keys in the lock. "We have to call the police," Suzanne said.

Frieda's voice rose with panic. "They'll put me away."

"We'll say it was self-defense."

The two women froze with fear when they heard Rick in the hallway.

"Suzanne," he called out to her. "That had better not be Lyon's car outside." He came into the living room and halted at the sight before him. He didn't say anything, but his dark penetrating glance darted between the two women, asking questions they were both afraid to answer.

After a long tense moment, Suzanne took a step toward him and said, "I can explain."

He folded his arms. "Then start talking—fast."

She told him about how he'd left his cell phone behind and how she'd tricked Wallace with a text message. She told him about her attempts to deceive Wallace into telling her the information he was using to blackmail Rick. Then she told him about the tape and the struggle.

"That's when I came in," Frieda said. "He was hurting her and I had to stop him."

Rick held his forehead. "With a tire iron?"

Frieda ran up to him and grabbed the front of his shirt her eyes filled with misery. "I had to do it," she said in a low voice only he could hear. "He was trying to destroy our family. He was going to tell her the truth about everything and I couldn't let him."

He tenderly covered the hands grasping his shirt. "Momma, do you know what you've done?"

"We have to call the police," Suzanne said.

"Not until we get our stories straight."

"Our stories are straight. It was self-defense."

"A good prosecutor can argue that it was murder. He was blackmailing us. That's a good reason to kill him."

"I'll just explain—"

Rick shook his head, disregarding her words. "Stop being naive. This is Anadale and a lousy 'Gordon' just killed one of the town's important 'Lyons.' Don't forget what happened to Melba. Part of her sentence was because she was born on the wrong side of the tracks and tried to marry up. That's not done."

"That's only part of the reason. She shot—"

"A Lowell," Rick finished. "And she paid for it. Do you think that if she were some rich woman from the right family that she'd have gotten the same conviction? The prosecution won because of a smear campaign and character assassination from key people. It hadn't mattered that that bastard Lowell had beaten her for years and everyone knew it, but no one said anything.

"It's no different now. Everyone knows what Lyon is like, but the moment he becomes a victim, my mother's life doesn't mean anything. It's Us against Them."

"It's different now. You're rich and with the right lawyers—"

"It won't change anything. The law doesn't work for us! We're Gordons. Do you know how long they put my brother away for? Eighteen years. He stole a TV and computer from a house and got eighteen years. He didn't even use a weapon. Do you think that's fair?"

"No, but it was his second offense and—"

He raised his brows, amazed. "So that makes it right?"

"I didn't say that. It's just that the law—"

"That's right," Rick said in a satirical tone. "You know a lot about the law. You know how this justice system works. Your father was part of it."

Suzanne met his cold gaze and let herself finally speak the truth. "And you hated him."

"Yes, I did."

"And what did you do about it?"

"I—"

"Rick, don't," Frieda cried. "Please. Think about it. The moment she knows she'll leave us."

Rick kept his gaze on Suzanne. "She'll leave us anyway."

"No, she won't." Frieda turned to Suzanne and for a moment her liquid eyes reminded her of Luke's. "You won't, will you?"

"No," she told the older woman whom she'd grown to love as a mother. She raised her gaze to Rick's. "Not unless you want me to."

"You might change your mind when you hear what I have to say."

Frieda clasped her hands together as though in prayer. "Rick—"

"Quiet, Momma, she needs to hear this." He tapped his chest. "I'm the reason your father lost everything. His company was on shaky ground and I went in for the kill and left him with nothing. I wanted to get revenge for all the injustices he'd done and the ones I thought he'd done. And you were part of that plan, too. I was going to make you a Gordon and in the process erase the Rand name from Anadale history. And I was going to keep you in the dark as to the man you'd really married until Wallace told me that he knew what I'd done to your father. I was willing to pay whatever I needed to, so that you'd never find out."

"Because you were afraid I'd leave and take your money?"

"No," he said, but didn't offer more.

"But that's all changed now," Frieda said, eager to set things right. "We're different. We love you now. Don't we Rick?"

Suzanne turned to Rick, unable to breathe.

He didn't meet her gaze and made a motion of exasperation. "It doesn't matter, what matters is this damn body in our living room."

Her heart slowly cracked. "I have a solution," Suzanne said in a cool, quiet voice. She walked over and picked up the tire iron. "I'll call the police and tell them that I did it. And if I'm convicted of murder I'll be put away for life and your revenge against the Rands will be complete." She held Rick's gaze. "Then you don't have to worry about me divorcing you and taking your money and your mother will be safe. That's what matters, right?"

Rigid silence met her words. Frieda rushed over to her. "No, honey that's not what we want. I didn't plan it to be this way. I was protecting you, I swear. We're a family now and family takes care of each other and I was taking care of you. Tell her, Rick. Tell her that what she thinks about us is wrong."

"We can all run," Rick said.

Suzanne nodded. "You two can run and I'll stay here and take the blame." She reached for the phone.

He ripped it from her grasp. "Stop being an idiot."

"What do you care what I do?" she snapped. "What

I've done hasn't mattered before. Why should it now?" She gestured to the door. "Go. Run. Protect your mother and your name. I'm not leaving."

"She's right, Rick," Frieda said, resigned. "We can't run. We have to face up to this, at least I do. I'll tell them the truth. It's the right thing to do."

"You can't," he said with anguish. "They'll convict you."

"You don't know that," Suzanne said. "We'll hire the best attorneys and if this does go to trial we'll make sure it's set in another town. The law can work."

"We can get through this," Frieda added. She headed for the front door. "I need a smoke."

Rick watched his mother go, and then he hung his head and sighed. He stared at the phone and reluctantly held it out. "Call the police."

Chapter 18

The police promptly arrived and questioned them all. Suzanne, Rick and Frieda were put in separate rooms and gave their versions of events while the living room was corded off, photographed and studied as the potential crime scene it had become. Finally, Wallace's body was taken away and the police left. No charges were filed that night, but the detective in charge made it clear that he'd be talking to the trio again.

Later that evening, Rick sat in his study, nursing a glass of bourbon, trying to figure out how everything could have gone so wrong. For the first time in a long while he craved a cigarette, but then he thought about Luke and knew he'd never start that habit again.

Suzanne knocked on the door and entered, taking a

seat in front of him. "After some struggle, I finally got your mother to sleep."

Rick finished off his drink then set it down on the desk. "Good."

"I thought you didn't drink."

"So did I." He opened the bottom drawer of his desk where he hid his bourbon. "I'll move my things out of the room tomorrow."

"Why?"

Rick looked at her, surprised by the question. "You really have to ask me that? I destroyed your father and my mother just killed your ex-husband." He rested the bottle on his desk. "You're better off without us."

Suzanne leaned forward with dismay. "But you're all I have. You, Frieda and Luke are my family."

"No, we're not." He twisted the top of the bottle in an angry motion. "There are plenty of other Rands, your aunt for example. And you have your mother's family."

"I thought I was a Gordon. Or is that only when it's convenient to you?"

Rick poured himself another drink.

Suzanne reached out and picked up his glass. She swallowed its contents then defiantly set the glass down with a thud. "I'm stronger than you think." She slid the glass toward him. "And I can drink you under the table. It was a talent I learned while Wallace was out with other women."

"Are you offering me a challenge?"

"I'd rather go to bed."

"You should go."

"Not without you." She held out her hand. "Let's go to bed. We need the rest."

Rick looked at her hand then her face. "No." He lifted the glass and held it against his forehead, his voice weary. "I'm a bastard."

"Yes, you are a bastard," she agreed, surprising him. "You stole my heart and I didn't even care."

He set the glass down and sniffed. "So you think that you love me?"

"I know I do."

"How much?"

"What do you mean?"

He leaned back and watched her through half-closed eyes. "Unlike men, I know that women love in degrees—that they can burn hot and cold in an instant."

She leaned on the desk. "While some men hardly love at all."

"We're just more careful who we give our hearts to."

"Because you're scared."

He straightened. "Because we're more constant." He stood. "If I'd come back poor would you still love me?"

Misery fell on Suzanne like a steel weight as she looked at the defiance in his gaze. "You destroyed my father, watched him sell all the things I treasured, bought my house and tricked me into marriage for your revenge and you question how much I love you?" She pushed herself from the desk with fury. "You're a bigger bastard than I thought and any love that I have for you is wasted." She spun away and swung open the door.

He ran up to her and seized her arm. "I'm sorry," he said, his voice raw with emotion. When she wouldn't look at him, he lifted her chin. "Really." He sighed. "I just can't believe that you could forgive me. That you could love me, that you've ever loved me.

Women were always telling me that they loved me, but it wasn't true. But you..." He turned her around and stared at her with wonder. "I know I'm a bastard and I come from a long line of bastards and I don't deserve you, but I don't care." He took her mouth with savage intensity—his kiss unlike any before. It wasn't tender, it wasn't wild, it was possessive, demanding, eager. "I want you more than my next breath," he said.

"Then take me," she whispered back.

He ripped her clothes from her shoulders, ignoring the sound of tearing cloth, and in seconds she was naked and nothing else mattered except the magnificent man holding her in his arms. This time when he touched her, her body didn't tingle, it burned. He removed his own clothes and they fell to the floor, his mouth exploring her thighs then moving up. His wet tongue made entry and filled her with ecstasy. She soon returned the favor taking him into her mouth and teasing him with her tongue, his tormented groan a heady delight.

"You'd better stop," he said through clenched teeth, "or I'm going to come in your mouth."

"I don't mind."

"I do," he said and quickly changed their positions. Then he entered her and they both felt an explosive release that made them tremble. Suzanne cried out and Rick moaned and nothing else needed to be said as they took pleasure in each other. At last they collapsed, exhausted but exhilarated.

Rick rested on his side and outlined the tip of her breast. "Don't say you love me, just say you need me."

"No," she said, cupping the side of his face. "I love

you and I can't help it." She let her hand fall to his shoulder and cascade down his back until she felt one of his scars. "And I wish I had a magic wand and could make all your scars disappear."

"With you I forget that I have them, there's a special magic to that." He dropped a kiss on her nipple and whispered against her chest, "I'm no Robin Hood. Whatever I steal is mine." His eyes met hers. "And I won't let it go." His lips covered hers, slow and thoughtful.

And as he held her in his arms, tears of joy sprung to her eyes.

He drew away and rested his forehead against hers and murmured, "I can't believe this is happening again. Another murder in Anadale."

"The most they can charge your mother with is manslaughter," Suzanne said with confidence.

Rick shook his head. "No. They'll indict her and charge her with murder because of who she is. I saw how the detectives looked at her and me. It's like the past all over again. Nothing's changed."

"Yes, it has," Suzanne said, brushing her lips against his. "This time we're in it together."

Rick's words proved prophetic. Three weeks later as autumn slipped into winter, Frieda Gordon was indicted for first degree murder. The news put Anadale on the map and reporters swarmed the small town to follow the sensational story. Headlines such as Millionaire's Mother Charged with Murder and Bestselling Novelist's Mother-in-law Stands Accused were splashed across the front pages of newspapers both online and off, while TV reporters and cameras followed Rick's, Frieda's and Suzanne's every move. Claudia and Noreen offered their support through marathon phone call sessions and gift baskets to help Suzanne through this trying time. Suzanne's fans also came to her aid by sending hundreds of letters and e-mails telling her how much she meant to them. But all their efforts at comfort couldn't help the inevitable backlash.

Soon Suzanne and Rick were forced to take Luke out of school because kids relentlessly teased him about his grandmother going to jail and some parents didn't want their children associating with him. Mrs. Perigene found the stress of the situation too much and resigned. To protect Luke, Rick and Suzanne enrolled him in a private boarding school out of town.

In town, battle lines were drawn straight down socio-economic lines—the haves and the have-nots— and Rick and Suzanne were caught in the middle. They stayed home as much as possible and 468 Trellis Court became a prison instead of a haven. Even after the police had allowed them to clear up the crime scene, nobody stepped into the living room again. Suzanne didn't think the situation could get any worse until she woke up one day and discovered that Frieda was gone. She hadn't slept in her bed and had left a note telling them that they were better off without her. Suzanne quickly called Rick and he came home immediately. When he looked over the note, he swore.

"We can't call the police," Suzanne said as they sat in the kitchen wondering what they should do next.

Rick held his head. "That woman's going to drive me crazy."

"I don't think she's gone far. She just seemed to want to get away. Do you know of any place she might go to escape?"

He lifted his head. "If she ever wanted to escape she just picked up a whiskey bottle."

Suzanne frowned. "This is serious."

"I'm being serious. She'd drink and talk about…" He let out a fierce sigh. "I think I know where she is." He jumped to his feet. "Let's go."

Moments later Rick drove up to his old house, which looked abandoned and sad like a beat-up dog. The shingles on the roof were curling while the roof itself sunk forward toward the unkempt yard. Rick turned off his engine and stared at the structure. It was a house of anger and fear. A place where he and his brother would hide in the closets when his father got in one of his moods. A place where he'd have to sleep in layers of clothes in the winter and suffocate in the sweltering heat during the summer. He remembered being hungry, but mostly he remembered his father's fists. He briefly shut his eyes.

"Do you want me to go in?" Suzanne said gently.

Rick opened his eyes. "No, I'm okay." He took a deep breath then got out of the car and headed toward the house. When he opened the door he fought the weight of emotion that nearly crushed him. Part of him didn't want Suzanne to see where he'd grown up. It was a symbol of how different their lives were. But when he glanced at her he didn't see judgment or pity, just an overwhelming sadness. Yes, everything about this house was sad, but the past didn't matter right now. "Momma?" he called out into the dank hallway where the floorboards buckled.

Suddenly Frieda appeared. "You shouldn't have come here." She frowned when she saw Suzanne. "And you shouldn't have brought her."

"We're here to take you home."

"Just leave me here." She held out her hands, motioning to the dank walls. "This is where I belong. Not in that nice place you got for me, or that fine house you live in, but here." She hugged herself. "I've ruined everything for you, Rick. Every time you've had a chance at happiness I've gotten in the way."

"That's not true."

"It is true."

Suzanne pushed past Rick and held her hand out to Frieda. "Momma, we need you at home with us. Please."

Frieda stared at Suzanne's outstretched hand and tears fell down her cheeks. "You called me momma."

"Yes, because you are."

"And you need me?" she said, unsure.

Suzanne nodded. "Now come."

Frieda looked at Rick. "Is this really what you want?"

He took his mother's hand. "I wouldn't want anything else. We're going to fight this."

Rick hired top lawyers, Timothy Yand and Melissa Banks out of Raleigh, to handle his mother's case, and Suzanne's knowledge about the importance of gathering and putting together a powerful case was of great help to them. She told them about Wallace's violent behavior when they were married and his corrupt business practices. Although the lawyers hadn't been able to get the trial set in a different location, they'd been able to convince a judge to let them select jurors from another county. As the court date loomed closer, tension between Rick and Suzanne grew.

"Thank you," Rick said to Suzanne one night as they lay in bed staring up in the darkness. The winter wind howled outside their window.

"For what?"

"The way you handled my momma when she ran away."

"She's my momma, too."

He laughed.

"What's so funny?"

"The way you say it. It sounds so proper."

"I don't care. I like saying it. I wasn't allowed to growing up."

"You weren't?"

"Absolutely not," she said with mock horror. "I was a Rand. We didn't have mommas we had mothers."

Rick laughed again then sobered. "What do you think is going to happen?"

"What do you mean?"

"If you were to write this story, how would you make it end?"

"You know how I would end it."

Rick rested a hand behind his head. "Tell me anyway."

Suzanne turned on her side and stared at his profile. She couldn't see much in the darkness but the faint moonlight allowed her to see the shadow of his face. She knew he didn't believe the trial would go well and needed her reassurance. "At the end of *my* story, Frieda will be found 'not guilty' and all the people Wallace used and blackmailed will come forward and treat her as a hero and the Gordon name will become synonymous with honest justice."

"Your father wouldn't like that," Rick said with a smile in his voice.

"I don't care. This is my story." She placed a hand on his bare chest and could feel his heart beating. "The lawyers are putting together a very powerful argument. I've been working closely with them and they're going to poke holes in the prosecutor's case. You don't need to worry so much."

"The prosecutor knew Wallace. They were good friends. He's going to go for the kill."

"Everyone knew Wallace and I know how the prosecution works and so do Tim and Melissa."

"He's still confident. I've read his statements to the press."

"He has to be. Law is all about appearances, but we're going to win."

Rick wanted to believe her, but he was afraid. How could their marriage last the strains of this trial? What would happen if his mother was convicted? Could Suzanne stand being married to a man with two family members in prison? How would the people of Anadale treat her? Could she continue to weather this storm? He turned on his side, but couldn't sleep.

Suzanne couldn't sleep, either, her own fears making that impossible. She knew Rick cared for her, but he loved his mother. There was a bond she couldn't compete with and in a way she was still an outsider. Rick loved his mother and his son, but she was just his wife, something he could easily discard. She wasn't a part of him like they were. What if the prosecution won? What if Melba happened all over again? Suzanne squeezed her eyes closed. No, she couldn't imagine that. She slipped out of bed and left the room. She went into the family room and picked up her violin case and held it close, thinking about Melba and her mother. Tears filled her eyes.

She wished she could talk to them now. She'd never felt so alone. What if she did everything she could for Frieda and failed? Would Rick blame her? Would he hate her for giving him hope when there wasn't hope at all?

"I thought I heard movement out here?" Neena said coming into the room.

Suzanne set the violin case down and quickly wiped her eyes. "I was just sitting here."

"And worrying."

"Yes," Suzanne admitted. "I've told Rick so many things that might not be true. I've used words to make him feel better, but what if I'm wrong and he despises me later?"

"He won't, but if he does, he's a fool. But I seriously doubt that." Neena gave her a hug. "Your words mean a lot to him. They mean a lot to all of us."

Suzanne brushed her words aside with a shake of her head. "It's not me. It's just something my mother taught me about the power of words and seducing men."

Neena smiled. "The difference between you and your mother is that you mean every word you say. You don't talk to Rick just to soothe his ego. Your words come from the heart and that's what keeps him under your spell." Her smile widened. "But don't ever let him know that."

"But—"

"You're doing everything right." She rested her hand on top of Suzanne's. "You've made mistakes, but, my dear, you're not perfect and that's okay. Your parents are dead and so are their high standards. Do your best. That's all anyone can expect. Now go back to bed before your husband misses you. Everything is going to be fine."

Suzanne straightened, feeling the strength of Neena's words. "I believe you."

A week later, Suzanne wasn't as confident as she sat in the crowded courtroom and heard the prosecutor's opening argument. She looked at the faces of the jurors—five women and seven men of different races and ages—and could see them falling under his seductive spell. He was an impressive presenter who painted Frieda as a conniving woman, with one son in prison and a lout of a husband in the grave, who'd killed Wallace because he was a threat to her livelihood—her son Rick. Frieda's senior attorney, Melissa, refuted this picture. She was an imposing figure who stood five-eleven with streaks of silver in her black hair and a commanding voice, but Suzanne could see that the jurors weren't as easily swayed by her. After the first day, Suzanne met alone with Melissa at a restaurant outside of town. "How did you feel today went?"

"It's still early," Melissa said, stirring several spoonfuls of sugar into her coffee.

"Tell me the truth."

She sighed. "It's an uphill battle. Frieda's background is a problem. She has a record. Those who can vouch for her also have records."

"But Della will speak for her."

Melissa sipped her drink. "Della's testimony will help, but it won't be enough." She placed her coffee down. "I won't lie to you. This is not going to be an easy case. We'll have to fight all the way and the outcome will be anyone's guess."

"But you already think you know what it will be," Suzanne said, reading Melissa's face.

"We're going to need a miracle." Her cell phone rang and she glanced at the number. "It's from Timothy. Excuse me." She left the table to answer the phone. Minutes later she returned with a puzzled look.

"What's wrong?" Suzanne asked.

"I'm not sure. Timothy said he just got a strange call."

"From whom?"

"The woman didn't leave her name, but she did say we should call the M.E."

The medical examiner was an average-size Asian-American man with thinning hair and bushy eyebrows who welcomed Timothy, Melissa and Suzanne into his office with a warm grin.

"I don't usually do this," he said after they were seated, "but I don't believe this case should be going to trial."

Suzanne sat forward. "Why not?"

"I believe the police always do their best and with many cases they've learned to trust their instincts, but some times their instincts are wrong. Such as a case like this. When I first heard about how the decedent was found I understood why they came to the conclusion they did. That he died due to trauma from a blunt force object. However, it is my duty to look beyond the surface." He then began to explain what other evidence can be uncovered in an autopsy in such detail that Melissa was forced to interrupt him.

"Yes, that makes sense," she said. "But why are we here?"

"The blow from the tire iron was off center and graced the decedent's head. However, it did cause a lot of bleeding which would account for the police's conclusion that that's what killed him."

"But it didn't?"

"No. He had an aneurysm. That's what killed him."

They stared at him. Then Timothy said, "Are you saying that the aneurysm killed him and not the head trauma?"

"Yes."

"But the prosecution could argue that the hit on the back of the head caused the aneurysm," Melissa said.

The M.E. firmly shook his head. "No, the blow wasn't strong enough. Now had a healthy man swung the iron, yes considerable damage could have occurred and you'd have a hard case, but the person who created this injury did not have the strength to kill him."

Suzanne turned to the attorney. "Rick once told me that his mother had suffered a TIA, a ministroke, and that had left her dominant hand a little weak."

The M.E. nodded. "That explains it."

"And you're willing to testify?" Melissa asked.

"Yes."

"Could another pathologist dispute this?"

He shrugged. "Maybe. I know that the prosecution

already plans to have an out of state expert come up with another angle, but they'd have to pay someone a lot of money to disregard the facts. But when I told the prosecution—"

"They knew about this and didn't tell us?" Melissa interjected.

"That's what bothered me. I'd expected your call and never got one. When I talked to the judge—"

"Which judge?" Suzanne asked.

"Not the one presiding over the case," the M.E. said quickly. "Just a friend of mine. I call her 'the judge' out of affection, but I'd rather not tell you who she is."

Suzanne nodded, but could hazard a guess. It would be just like Jean to send an anonymous call.

"Doesn't matter," Melissa said. She turned to Suzanne with a triumphant grin. "We just got our miracle."

Before the presiding judge started the continuation of the trial the defense requested a meeting in his chambers and argued that the prosecution had suppressed evidence that clearly would have exonerated Frieda and prevented the trial. The judge readily agreed and after reprimanding the prosecution ordered the case against Frieda Gordon dismissed.

And just as quickly as they'd appeared, the reporters and cameras disappeared, and soon Anadale settled back into a quiet town once again and residents returned to their normal routine.

But Rick couldn't. He sat in his office still amazed by how events had turned out. One moment he was about to lose everything, then everything was okay again. Those who'd initially kept their distance now wanted to have lunch with him. But that didn't bother him. What amazed him was that the law had worked. For once in his life he felt that justice was real.

His phone rang and he picked up the receiver. "Yes?"

"You have a visitor," his assistant said.

"Fine." He cleared his desk and straightened as the door opened. His welcoming posture relaxed when he saw who it was—Jean, the judge who'd at first refused to let him marry Suzanne. She'd been cordial to him at the summer garden party, but the sting of her cruel words still remained. "How can I help you?" he said with cold politeness. He gestured to a chair. "Have a seat."

Jean glanced at the chair, but didn't sit. "You look as though you'd prefer to string me up and tell me to jump off a cliff than have me sit down."

"If you weren't my wife's friend I'd tell you a lot of things."

Jean nodded. "That's fair."

Rick clasped his hands together. "I'm a busy man, do I need to repeat my question?"

"No. I just wanted to stop by and say congratulations. I'm glad everything worked out for your family."

Her words surprised him, but he still kept his guard up. "Thank you."

Jean sighed. "There's a quote by Voltaire that I've always liked. 'We are all full of weakness and errors, let us mutually pardon each other our follies—it is the first law of nature.'" She held out her hand. "I was wrong about a lot of things and I'm sorry."

Rick looked at the offered hand, knowing how much humility and courage it took for her to come to him. He stood and shook her hand. "It's okay," he said with sincerity, letting his hatred for her melt away.

Jean tightened her grip then released her hold. "Thank you." He nodded and she turned. "Let me know when your brother is up for parole. Perhaps we can have him home by next Christmas."

"Momma would like that."

"But you don't think Suzanne will?"

"Let's just say it might make things awkward."

"Suzanne is a strong woman and, unlike her parents and some of her friends," Jean said with some chagrin, "she's not a snob and she'll stay by you no matter what. This last trial opened up a lot of old wounds in this town again, but it also healed some. Perhaps in the future we won't be so quick to judge each other."

"I hope so."

"Me, too," Jean said, leaving.

Rick sat back in his chair and thought about the judge's words. Had things really changed in Anadale now? Could his brother come home and not be seen as a degenerate Gordon, but rather a man who'd made mistakes and needed redemption? Could he raise his son to be proud of being a Gordon rather than the stepson of a Rand? Could Suzanne live in peace now instead of in the chaos that always seemed to surround his life? He rested his head back and imagined their future life together.

Miles away Suzanne imagined their lives apart. The events of the past several weeks had changed her. She stood outside 468 Trellis Court and stared at the snow covering the rooftops and railings like extra frosting on a cake. She watched Frieda and Luke, who was on winter holiday, build a snowman off to the side and knew that Neena would soon call them inside for dinner.

It was a beautiful image of home and family, but she

felt as though she was staring at it through a looking glass as an outsider. She couldn't be part of that picture because she knew she could no longer live there. To her the house held too many painful memories—arguments with her father, the tears she'd shed over Melba's trial, Wallace's death, and how it had been like a prison during Frieda's trial. Suzanne knew she could never find happiness there.

She had to leave it and the town, even if it meant losing all that she'd come to love. Her heart ached with pain. She knew that she would be leaving by herself because Rick loved the town in spite of its flaws and he'd worked all his life to own 468 Trellis Court. He needed the house, not her.

"Don't scream," a deep voice said from behind her.

Suzanne's heart leaped with delight at the sound of his voice and she spun around. She saw Rick looking very much the self-made success he was, wrapped in a dark blue cashmere coat and matching scarf. He looked worlds apart from the jeans-clad man who'd reappeared in her life months earlier. But she knew they'd both changed. "I didn't hear you drive up," she said.

"You were lost in thought," he said.

"Yes," she agreed. "You're home early."

"I wanted to surprise you." He pulled out a brochure and handed it to her.

Suzanne opened it up and stared at the stunning colonial house portrayed and its many rooms and enormous property. "What's this?"

"I thought it could be our new home."

She looked up at him, startled. "What?" She glanced

at the house behind her then stared at him with confusion. "I thought this was what you wanted."

"No," he said softly, his eyes melting into hers. "I'm looking at what I've always wanted. I just didn't know it at the time."

Suzanne gripped the brochure in her fist as tears gathered in her eyes. She stared at him speechless.

"I wasn't going to pay Wallace the blackmail money, but I was willing to do whatever I needed to in order to make sure you never found out the truth because I didn't want to face losing you. I love you. I don't think I ever stopped and I tried." His voice grew rough. "God, did I try, but I couldn't stop. You once accused me of stealing your heart, but you stole my very soul. Forever and always I will be whoever you need me to be—whether it is your protector, your friend or your lover. I won't let anyone hurt you." He cradled her face in his hands. "You're safe now."

Safe. She'd never felt safe before. Not with a man. With her father it had always been a battle. With Wallace it had been a game. With John, her agent, it had been betrayal. From Melba to her mother she'd learned that men weren't to be trusted, that they only broke your heart. But this time as she looked into Rick's eyes her heart knew he spoke the truth.

"I know."

"I've lied about some things, but never how I feel about you. When I read your book I saw that you didn't let the Melba character die in the end. She got paroled and started a new life and had a bright future."

"I wanted her to have a happy ending."

"But you didn't give Donna and Roland one. Roland

eventually leaves Donna and we don't know what happens to him and she decides to never love again."

Suzanne glanced away and saw a sparrow sitting on the bare branch of a tree in the distance as she thought about the sad ending for the two lovers. "It seemed the right ending at the time."

"Do you think they'll get a second chance?"

She looked at him, unsure. "I don't know."

"What about us? Do you think you can give us a happy ending?"

Suzanne bit her lip, the winter air chilling her tears. A happy ending? Did they happen outside of books? Could she allow herself to believe in them? She turned to Frieda and Luke who were now throwing snow at each other, the white powder glistening like diamonds in the sun. Then she stared down at the brochure in her hand and all the possibilities it offered. She looked up at Rick.

He was a man women found deliciously appealing; the man some men trusted and others feared. Suzanne realized she had come to love these attributes instead of despising them. A woman's second glance didn't bother her anymore because she trusted him. People's prejudices were no longer an issue because she knew the truth—that he was solid and fair and generous. She'd come to adore his sly grins and intense eyes, his dark secrets and tender heart. She loved him with every fiber of her being and this time the thought didn't terrify her at all.

Suzanne put her arms around Rick's neck and pressed her mouth against his, exploring the velvety warmth of his lips that made her forget the cold winter frost. When she drew away she caressed his cheek and said, "No, I can't give us a happy ending because we're not ending anything. We're at the beginning of our story and it begins with 'Once upon a time…'"

Claudia Madison was on her first cup of coffee when she checked her e-mail and saw Suzanne's message. She quickly read it then called Noreen Webster.

"Yes, I read it," Noreen said before Claudia could say anything.

Claudia laughed. "This would be perfect for one of your books."

"Almost too perfect," Noreen said, ever cautious. She cupped her chin in her hand and again read the note she'd just printed, unable to stop a smile.

Hello you two!
Right now I'm in Bermuda and as I sit next to my mother-in-law on the beach (I've taught her to crochet to keep the agility in her hands) and watch my husband and son in the distance, I know that true love is sweeter the second time around. So I tell you, my dearest friends—continue to write, continue to laugh and continue to love. It's definitely worth the risk.
Suzanne